WINNING

THE

CITY

Theodore Weesner

SUMMIT BOOKS

NEW YORK   LONDON   TORONTO   SYDNEY

TOKYO   SINGAPORE

SUMMIT BOOKS
Simon & Schuster Building
Rockefeller Center
1230 Avenue of the Americas
New York, New York 10020

Designed by Caroline Cunningham
Manufactured in the United States of America

1   3   5   7   9   10   8   6   4   2

Library of Congress Cataloging in Publication Data

Weesner, Theodore.
Winning the city / Theodore Weesner.
p.   cm.
Summary: A fifteen-year-old boy who dreams of winning the city
league basketball tournament finds out how unfair life can be.
[1. Basketball—Fiction.]   I. Title.
PS3573.E36W5   1990
813'.54—dc20
[Fic]   90-9474
                                                                       CIP
                                                                        AC

ISBN 0-671-64241-3

Permission for the use of lyrics on page 29 from "Paper Doll" by Johnny
Black has been granted by the Edward B. Marks Music Company.

For Janet

PART ONE

This was it. Today. The first practice of the season was scheduled to take place after school. Time to do the deed.

All these months he had been able to think of little else. Since last spring. It was his year, his time to be the oldest, and now it was here. Practice today. Tryouts. But he was a returning starter and he sure wasn't trying out; he was leading the way. His excitement was such that all day he had been telling himself to be cool. Cool was the way to be. Time to be cool and not a fool.

Dale Wheeler was fifteen, though, and however he tried to maintain that certain temperature, he did not know how not to dream. He had grown an inch and a half since last year and he was growing right now. This very moment he was pushing up through five-nine. Sitting at his desk in school, he could look at a forearm and see it growing larger, stronger, longer. He could call up his arm muscles at home before the bathroom mirror. One, then the other. Pop, pop! Pow, pow! He could call up excitement within, too, in the approximate location of his heart.

Dale knew he was good. And there was no doubt he had worked. Like a saver saving every penny, he had given himself to little else. At times it seemed it was all he had done, all this time, work-work, practice-practice. He had worked on anyway. Worked into work. Sweated into sweat. Work was commitment. Work, as every athlete knew, was the key. The more you practice, the luckier you get. He had done it, was doing it, would do it. An athlete was what he was. Maybe he was only fifteen years old, but he knew what he was. And now it was his year, it was his turn to take all of them downtown to win the City. "Here comes Dale Wheeler," said the Sportscaster in the sky. "There he goes . . . he takes the shot, he fakes the shot, he drives! he shoots! he SCORES!!"

Even asleep at night Dale dreamed of the season to come. Moments and moves from outdoor pickup games earlier in an evening—spectacular things happened in pickup games—would blend in his dreams into the season to come, to games indoors before bleachers filled and rocking with all the students and teachers he had ever known or passed in the hallways of Whittier Junior High. Waking from a dream he would feel strangely filled with rainbows. Don't go off the deep end, he had to remind himself. Be cool. Cool is cool. Don't be a fool—play it cool.

Everything's a game. He knew that. Life, he told himself with clarity, is a game. It's a game all the way, and everything depends on how you play it. It was something he *knew*. He had no notion of himself as any kind of thinker, nor as a smartass fifteen-year-old either—not yet—but he knew what he knew and he knew by now that life was a game.

"There he goes . . . ," said the Sportscaster in the sky.

One night during the summer his father came in late from working second shift at Chevrolet Plant Four—a silhouette in Dale's bedroom doorway; a weaving silhouette for sure, as per usual—and invited him to the kitchen for a middle-of-the-night snack of Coney Island hot dogs. That night, as on most other nights during the summer, Dale had played outdoors at the park until the lights had gone off at ten, had dribbled the mile home on dark sidewalks, in and out of corner street lights, had showered with the landlady's garden hose in the basement, had fallen asleep easily and slid into the dreaming of his dream. There came the figure of his father, the tender words, hey son, old sleepytime pal, Coney Island dogs. They had to be the best hot dogs in the world, and middle-of-the-night snacks were his father's way of telling him he liked him, loved him, they were father and son, pals in the face of all obstacles and until the end of time. Dale mumbled that he'd be out in a minute.

Then sunlight was filling his window and it was time to get up—to return to the park for a day of practice—even as a spur of something was picking at his mind. Slipping into the bathroom to wash and brush his teeth, he heard music—"Slipping Around," Margaret Whiting and Jimmy Wakely circling on his father's old phonograph in the living room—and Dale was stopped as he always was by music drifting through their handful of second-floor rooms at an odd hour. The message was familiar; his father was up and sloshed, sweet and sentimental, drunk and dangerous. Waiting for his son to appear, for there was no one else upon whom to visit his love and pain, his loss and regret.

Dale had no choice, finally, but to leave his bedroom and make his way into the kitchen.

Curly Wheeler stood there. He wasn't sitting, as Dale had expected, but, on his feet, was leaning against the wall. He looked as if he had been leaning there all night. His neck seemed made of rubber as he rolled his head to take a look at his son, to say, "Don't I know you from somewhere?"

Dale opened the refrigerator door, explored the chances for breakfast, generally ignored his father, as he did at times like this. Life with an alcoholic.

"YOU'RE the guy who stood me up!" his father announced. "That's who you are. You're that guy! Bring home a special meal for the only person in the world who plays tunes on his weary old heartstrings—in the middle of the night—guy gets left standing on the corner."

Dale had remembered by then. "My gosh, I went back to sleep!" he said. "I fell asleep."

"Musta been dreaming about something a hell of a lot better-looking than Coney Island hot dogs," his father said with a grin.

"Basketball," Dale said, deciding all at once to take a chance on the truth. "I was dreaming about basketball."

"Basketball?" his father said. "You said basketball? Did you say basketball?"

"This is my big year," Dale said.

"Well, what's that mean? First time I knew anything would keep you away from your favorite meal. Figured it had to be something a lot prettier than some fat old basketball."

"It's my big year at school coming up," Dale said. "I've been working like a demon. Everybody else is just doing nothing. I've been working all the time. All summer. It's my big year—we're gonna win the City." He did not add how proud he hoped to make his father, how he dreamed of saving their lives in some small way. Turning things around. Leading them both to some promised land.

His father was squinting at him, closing one eye. "Son, goddam, gotta tell you one thing. Hope you dream about other things, too. You hear me talking? Don't wanna put all your eggs in one little basket, do you?"

Dale nodded, to say, well, he knew, he was cool, he knew.

Of course, he did not know, and anticipation remained his closest companion. Even when school was under way in the fall and he wanted to do homework—or just think about something else, anything else, of the day's Word

Power Challenge in homeroom, of Zona Kaplan sitting in front of him—some basketball moment, comments from the Sportscaster in the sky, a make-believe sports page headline from the season to come would slip into his mind on its own, would present itself as irresistibly as a puppy eager to play. Go on, get out of here, he'd tell the pup, but she'd keep snuggling, playful as a girlfriend he had never had, licking his face, smiling and breathing into his ear as she unbuttoned her blouse and let fall free those items his father thought not unreasonable competition for Lower Downtown's famous Coney Island natural casing hot dogs smothered in their secret recipe chili sauce.

Be cool, Dale kept telling himself. Don't go off the deep end. One step at a time. Put it together. Don't be a jerk— do the work!

He had done the work, however, had worked to put it together, and the flame which burned within seemed to be his to claim. The previous day after school he had practiced yet again on the outdoor court at the park. No one else was there. For sure. For no one worked like he worked. None of them knew commitment like he knew commitment. He rehearsed his moves, took his shots, dreamed his dream until the air was chilled and the ball was a black moon against the lowering autumn sky. He worked into the dark. Get outta the way, he told the invisible opposition. Get outta the way, here comes Wheeler and he came to play.

And that very morning at seven, sweeping his school's two gyms—as he did every morning, in exchange for time on the floor—he had jumped, checked with his eye, pulled the trigger a hundred times or more, shot free throws for five minutes, too, made himself make five in a row, then five more, then five more, before hurrying into the hallway at the last second to join the sleepyheads (they would fill the stands when the season was under way) who were just wandering into the building for the start of the school day and had no idea at all about commitment or that life was a game and everything had to do with how it was played.

Oh, it was his year and he was more than ready. To say the least, as Zona Kaplan, as all the girls in his ninth grade class seemed to say. A flame of desire burned within him. To say the least.

There all at once was Sonny Joe Dillard, the school's star, its legendary athlete, walking in the other direction, not hurrying at all. "I have a name for City League!" Dale said.

"What's the name, Wheels?"

"Not gonna say right now," Dale said. "Tell you later."

"What if we don't like it, Wheels?"

"You'll like it. We'll like it."

"Thought we were going to get a sponsor this year, Wheels."

"Aah! You have to go around begging people. That's a drag. Who needs it."

"Tell me at practice," Joe said, ambling on his way.

"What practice—what're you talking about?"

"Yeah, as if you didn't know," Joe called back. "Tell me at practice, Wheels."

"Everything in due time, Joe," Dale called after him.

This was it. It was starting right now. Dressed way ahead of the others, the old tingle of goose bumps alive on his naked legs, Dale left the locker room and passed through the brief tunnel into the boys' gym. Before him, however, was a modest surprise. The wall between the two gyms was folded away. The last two years they had used the boys' gym alone for the first and all other practices. Now it was different. Before him was the great sweep of the double gym, and Dale asked himself in passing what it was that Coach Burke was up to this year.

No matter and about five-eight, he thought as, continuing into the vast space, new tingles of goose bumps traversed his legs and forearms, ran over his bare shoulders and into his faintly smiling face.

Each of the two courts was full size, but when the floor-to-ceiling panels were folded away and the larger backboards on either end were lowered and locked into place, as they were now, and when light from the entire line of high windows was allowed to reflect upon the whiskey-colored floor, then Dale might find himself moved in a way that some other person might be moved by the cavernous silence and stained glass of a cathedral. The future was in his hands.

Then, oh God, for an instant the old painful incident of seventh grade stabbed him. He should have known. It was always returning to stab him—his father coming that one time to see him play, for some reason not working second shift that day, coming that one time and losing a leg through the bleachers, losing a bottle from his coat pocket, too, a bottle in a brown paper bag that fell through the planks of wood, hit the floor and broke, and kids, and teachers and parents, too, said, "Who's that man?" and "He lost his bottle!" and "Look at that guy—he's half in the bag!"

Dale moved a little, shook out his arms and legs to loosen up, to think of something else. He raised his arms, went to his toes, fired an imaginary shot with his fingers. Another. The future was right there in his hands.

"Belly high . . . without a rubber," he sang aloud, to get himself further away from the old bugaboo thought of his father. The lyric was one he had dared recite to Zona in homeroom two mornings ago, and she had raised her eyes in disgust. "Ninth grade boys are so immature," she said at last, and Dale had liked her even more than he had liked her before. She seemed to bounce in his heart. To say the least.

He walked on, looking to the vast cathedral space of the empty double gym. He shot imaginary shots at other baskets.

Oh, this is like love, he thought in his silly but cocky, not-so-silly frame of mind. This—is what love feels like. If you've done the work, he thought. It's what it feels like to sit in homeroom and have the hots all the time for Zona Kaplan. This. He shot again. "Shake Marilyn Monroe!" he sang out. "I'm gonna shake . . . Marilyn Monroe!"

There were the tighter, heavier nets on the two orange-rims, from which hemp cords he imagined emanating that sound which thrilled him so. For even in the gym when it was empty, and sometimes when the bleachers were full, and certainly in his continuing dream—in a sport in which to practice is to dream—he could call into his ears that most reassuring of sounds. There would be this sudden stopping-pushing hard into the air, the certain gasp, the lining up, up-fixing of periscope, the hanging for an instant to aim, hanging unto the pulling of the trigger—fire one!—sending the ball tumbling through space, through momentary silence, through pause of heart and mind, too, arriving, alas, upon that snapping of nothing but threads (the "swish" that wasn't that at all), transmitting, delivering its payoff, the feeling within that said he was okay, yes, he was right with himself and with all things. He was real. He was good. He was. At least for the moment. *Whipp!* Two points! Score! All things on target at once and forever. *Whipp!* Take that, all you sonofabitches! Did you think Dale Wheeler did not come to play? Take that, world! *Whipp!* Take that and stick it up your ass, all of you! Dale Wheeler is here to do the job and the next time around you won't be laughing at his old man, because his old man won't be doing anything anymore to be laughed at. Never again.

Without a ball, Dale jumped again, aimed, popped again. Dreamed.

"Wheels, what're you doing?" a voice called behind him.

Dale looked over. Thinking it would sound clever, he called to the boy, a third-stringer at best, "Getting ready to win the City!"

"You bet!" the boy called.

"Betcher sweet ass!" Dale called in turn.

"Mine ain't sweet!" the boy called.

"Mine is!" Dale called. "Be-bop-a-lulu, she's my baby!" he sang out a little crazily until he told himself yet again to take it easy. Don't be a fool—play it cool. One step at a time, sweet Jesus. One step at a time. Turn it all around.

The year was his, but of course it was theirs, too, the others who were in their last year of junior high, and certainly the school's best-known athlete and biggest star, Sonny Joe Dillard. Scholastic Conference, for which this practice had been called, was fun and important, still it was City League, which did not start for three more weeks, that was the stage for the greater, fiercer competition, and called up their real dreams of fulfillment and glory.

Whittier Junior High was expected to win the year's Scholastic Conference going away. Made up of the city's five junior highs, its schedule included home and away games with the other four schools in a season of merely eight games. There were neither playoffs nor tiebreakers, and the season ended in early February, often upon the declaration not of a champion but of co-champions. Oh, they'd win the School League, Dale thought. Unless he and Sonny Joe both got hit by a truck. "Wheeler, Wheeler, he's our man!" the string of cheerleaders would sing in harmony. Still it was City League, it was the City, which was the object of all their dreams.

Districts, playoffs, and a sixteen-game regular season distinguished City League. Playoffs were the key. They offered excitement and sometimes magic. Teams which won their districts and progressed through the playoffs to the finals downtown in the City Auditorium, in March, would play nineteen games. Teams with names of the players' invention entered from all the towns in the county and from the city's private and parochial schools, too, drawing upon a student body four or five times that of the junior high conference alone. Crowds became large and intense by the end of the regular season, and in March, when the weather broke and the finals were on downtown in the City Auditorium— where the city high schools played their regular games and Dale had yet to shoot a single shot, where General Motors put on its New Car Show and Ringling Brothers Barnum & Bailey put up its nets when the circus came to town— it was as if nothing else was happening in the world and the hazed excitement filling the air, for those who made it, was the reward at the end of a first big-deal dream ever come true.

Yes, Dale thought. It was what he was doing. Getting ready to win the City. His dream was genuine, too, he knew, because it was more than possible that they'd pull it off; it was probable, as everyone knew. It was their year. The Blue Arrows. It was the name—as all but acknowledged captain—he had in mind for this year's team, the name he'd move his team adopt. The Blue Arrows.

"Ladies and gentlemen . . . The Blue Arrows! Winners of this year's city championship . . . captained by . . ."

"Be-bop-a-lulu, she's my baby!"

The Blue Arrows. Dale was in love with the name. He loved it so much that, like other items of anticipation, he could not wait to present it to his teammates. Still, he had held back, for at other times he was less certain of the name. Cool was the thing. Stay cool. Be cool, he told himself. Everything in due time, as his father liked to say. One step at a time. And, well, okay, he wasn't exactly the captain, he thought to admit to some heavenly observer who was reminding him not to jinx himself. But he'd be co-captain, that was for sure, and at least they would say, "co-captained by . . ." Betcher sweet ass.

. . .

Others followed into the gym and then there was another small surprise. Coach Burke, carrying two new basketballs, one under each arm, was accompanied by an enormous, gray-haired man Dale had never seen before. The man may have been a mere six-six or six-seven, but in the midst of the eighth) and ninth-graders, and next to squat Coach Burke, he loomed as large as some giant from another world.

The man wore a gray sweatshirt above gray gabardine slacks whose cuffs touched upon what was at once the focal point about him: great white basketball shoes around which there ran, parallel to the floor, a thin red line of rubber just visible within layers of white. Dale had heard from his father enough times the old saw of shoes telling on the man, and these sneakers, it was clear, had things to say. White side-walls on a vintage Packard is what came to mind. White— faintly yellowed, maybe—and carefully aged. The shoes reeked of power. They were talking.

Dale moved with the others. Like nails drawn to a mag-net, they followed the two men. "Who's that?" was whis-pered here and there among them. No one seemed to know. The man's hair, salt-and-pepper gray, was full, and however old he may have been, he retained bulk and strength of a kind which appeared rust free, well tuned, powerful.

Sonny Joe Dillard was approaching then, apparently the last player to come through the tunnel. The tall, long-armed boy was pulling a sweatshirt over his head on the move. The school's most legendary athlete, Sonny Joe, fifteen, already six-four and growing, making him the tallest ninth grader in the city's five-team school league, may have been the tallest fifteen-year-old in the entire county, with its population of more than half a million.

As Sonny Joe joined the gathering, however, and came

into proximity with the massive stranger, he looked, in his lesser width and bulk, more like a greyhound than a superstar.

Still—at least it was Dale's thought—Sonny Joe had to have something to do with the visit by the gray-haired horse in dress pants and white sidewalls. For just that previous August, after countless strikeouts and no-hitters as a left-hander in American Legion baseball—as if his fame as a basketball player were not enough—Joe Dillard had been offered, and had turned down, as they all knew, a $25,000 signing bonus by the Detroit Tigers. To sign would have made him ineligible thereafter for school sports, and given the "Bonus Baby Rule," he would have been obligated to go directly to the Major League club without benefit of time in the minors. Newspaper articles, and rumor, too, had it that the Tigers believed Joe Dillard could be the next Bob Feller and, when the signing bonus was turned down, that in a year or two, barring injury, the amount could be three times, four times, five times as great.

Dale, for his part, had given up on baseball altogether that summer. It wasn't that he disliked the sport, for it had been his first sports infatuation, and he loved it still. Nor was it that he had batted any number of times against Sonny Joe—perhaps forty, in City League Midget, Class E and D—and had to his credit but one clean, memorable hit, a triple between left and center, a few scratch singles, a couple walks, and thirty-some strikeouts, concentrated, hard-eyed swings at a Ping-Pong ball object fired from a rifle that seemed always to arrive in the catcher's mitt an instant before his bat cleared the plate.

Basketball came along and swept him off his feet. In baseball, well-oiled glove and cleats on the handlebars of his bicycle, hat beautifully crowned, wanting badly to play, he had ridden all around the city over several summers, and only rarely found anything other than someone else's organized game merely to watch, in addition to the two games, sometimes three, his own team might play each week. After the first warm days of spring almost no one ever wanted to play baseball, not even flies out or catch. And lobbing a taped ball onto a garage roof, to position himself under it as it rolled off, and fielding grounders on the rebound from a brick wall at school, generated next to nothing from the Sportscaster in the sky.

The key thing in basketball was that he could play alone, and the sport took him in as if he were a starving orphan. Ball in hand, anytime, anywhere, was a game. To shoot was to play, and to play was to dream. And unlike baseball, others came to play basketball in gangs and carloads. He could go to the park every day all summer, Dale learned, and shoot all day, by himself if necessary, however much the sun might blaze down upon the asphalt court. Then at dusk, always, players began to arrive, in cars, walking, on bicycles, and intensely competitive half-court games of three-on-three got going, and if your threesome did not lose, you could play for hours. Lights were turned on at eight, and in July and August a full-court Summer League ran until eleven every night, a league which attracted the city's best high school players, and college players, too, from city and state colleges. Crowds and girls came to strut and watch, to flirt and laugh and hang out, to sit in temporary bleachers, to stand around on the grass. And, as a park rat, Dale usually slipped on a striped shirt and whistle, to referee games made up of high school stars or college players, when, during time-outs and at halftime, he could put up a string of shots of his own and, as it occasionally happened, hear some spectator call out, "HEY, SIGN UP THE REF, HE'S BETTER THAN ANY OF YOU."

. . .

With a tweet of his whistle, Coach Burke quieted the group, drew its attention. He bounce-passed one of the new balls to Sonny Joe, the other to Dale.

"This year," Coach Burke said, "in case you've forgotten. This year is our year!" He paced a couple steps, as if considering what to say next and added, "Go ahead, sit down."

Sitting, Dale knew, wasn't for their comfort, but so the short, stocky man could gaze out upon them. Dale knew, too, that the balls had been entrusted to him and Sonny Joe as designated co-captains, that they were expected to hold them while Coach Burke paced and used his hands to talk. What Dale also knew in this moment—awareness swept up through him in one of those rainbow sensations— was pride in being so recognized. He and Sonny Joe. Returning starters from last year. Co-captains. They were the best players, as everyone knew. The good, satisfying sensation ran through his veins as he tried to get comfortable on the floor with the glossy new ball in his lap. It was his year; this was it.

What was also on his mind—as it had been, every day, all these months—was how surprised they were all going to be when they saw how much he had improved his game since last year. For he had not been lazy or complacent in any way as a returning starter. No way. He had gone for it. All summer, all fall, up through and including yesterday after school, unto darkness, and that very morning in the gym, he had done it. Practice, practice, practice, alone and with high school players, in the three-on-three half-court games, in Summer League games, playing as if each shot and each pass were for all time, incorporating unto himself the skills and moves he knew all along would leave these fourteen) and fifteen-year-olds, and Coach Burke, too, staring in amazement.

For "lazy" was their middle name, most of them, the rest of them, as everyone knew. What they had done was spend the summer days and weeks at lakes and cottages, at Yellowstone Park and Mackinac Island, lying in the sun. Sitting around and sleeping in, he imagined, which awareness had only urged him out earlier, driven him harder, and what he was feeling now, as Coach Burke rattled on about cleanliness and good citizenship in the locker room, was that in time, shortly, here at last, he was going to put on a display which would have even Sonny Joe, after his summer of countless strikeout fastballs, regarding him differently. Take the block! Shake the block! Fly through the air and make the shot! *"Double reverse lay-up with his left hand, ladies and gentlemen! Did you see that!? Did you see that shot!?"* Hey, look me over! This is my year!

Coach Burke was carrying on about these being tryouts and everybody having the same chance as everybody else, and Dale, his mind continuing to race and wander, could only think, oh, tell us all about it, Burkebutt. As Miss Turbush said in homeroom and in her math class, too, in this country a person who did the work might reap the reward. Anyone who paid the price might win the prize. Might turn things around. Betcher sweet ass.

Dale also wondered if he was being looked at—as a returning starter and co-captain, trusted guardian, too, of a glossy new ball—by the newcomers who were trying out for the senior team for the first time. Perhaps they knew and were thinking, that's Dale Wheeler and he came out for this team for the first time last year and became a starter in his first year! That's what he'd be thinking, Dale thought, if he were sitting there for the first time, although last year, he knew, what he had actually thought as he had looked over the competition had been more to the point of—I can beat any of you, and it's what I'm going to do, so get out of my way!

Dale made a decision then: He was going to sit on the new ball. He hardly hesitated. He *knew* Coach Burke would not berate him for it. And even as his seat on the ball put him a head higher than the others, he did it. It was done. He felt only slightly self-conscious in his raised position. He thought of his boldness and daring, here, and on the court in games, and he took pleasure in the gift he believed he had been granted. He was a leader.

It was why he was co-captain. They could go to their summer cottages, and be too lazy to practice in the blazing sun. They could chase girls all the time, too, and worry about clothes and their hair and tans. They could sit around and talk of how great they were going to be. But when the time came to win the City, well, they'd know where to turn and whose name to call. When the chips were on the line, when it was time to go downtown and winning was what they were after, they'd know whose name to call.

Dale seemed to feel as good in these moments as he had ever felt in his life. There was doing it versus not doing it, and he had done it. It was something, at last, that he knew. Perhaps it was the first thing he had ever known entirely on his own. He knew that it told on his manliness, too. His eyes glazed some, secretly, as he knew this. All summer, every night, he dreamed himself asleep on drives into the key and jumpers at the buzzer, on two-shot opportunities at the line trailing by one. But he had not known then what he knew he knew now, as he saw here the product, the payoff for his work and commitment, saw that it had given him this awareness that he had it, that he could do the job, that he was good.

"As for this year," Coach Burke was saying. "We have four returning lettermen and, for the first time ever, we have not one, but TWO returning starters, Joe Dillard and Dale Wheeler. Sonny Joe and Little Wheels. They are also this year's designated co-captains. Right now, though, without any further ado, what I want to do—before we start our first workout—is introduce to you a very special visitor who is with us today. Boys, the distinguished-looking gentleman beside me is none other than—Von Bothner."

The giant-size man took half a step forward and, like the pride of the Yankees, gave a slight nod.

"Well, I can tell that some of you might not recognize the name Von Bothner, so I'll have to fill you in a little. Von Bothner happens to be to basketball what Lynn Chadnois is around here to football. Mister Bothner was all-American at Niagara University in the not too distant past. I said all-American, in case you didn't hear me. And, for what, seven years, Von? For seven years he was the mainstay and starting center for none other than the Fort Wayne Zollner Pistons. Von Bothner kept up with his engineering studies as well, however, in college, and currently, if all that weren't enough achievement for one lifetime, he is Plant Supervisor, Chevrolet Plant Four.

"His sons," Coach Burke added, "who I imagine some of you HAVE heard of, are both very recent WINNERS of the Soap Box Derby. Keith, his oldest—I believe I have this right. Going to Akron, for the Nationals, two years ago, Keith finished SECOND in the entire country. That's in the entire United States of America. And last year Mr. Bothner's younger son, Karl, who was also the WINNER at the county level—Karl placed FIFTH overall in the Nationals at Akron!

"At any rate, you may not have known that we have so famous a basketball player living right on the outskirts of our own city—where, among all else this busy family keeps up with, in Fenton Meadows, they breed thoroughbred horses!

"So I'm certainly happy myself to have the opportunity to meet Mr. Von Bothner, to have a chance to chat with him, as I have this afternoon. And I'm pleased to have him join us today. Mr. Bothner's two sons will be coming into the city to school next year, one to high school, as I understand it, and one to our own Whittier Junior High, for which reason he is here today, to get a feel for the competition the city has to offer. So let's do our best, everybody, to see if we can show Mr. Bothner why it is that Whittier Junior High was city co-champion last year, and why it is that this year we have our sights set on going undefeated, on winning the Scholastic Conference title outright!

"First, though—don't get too anxious now. Before we start our first practice, I'm going to ask our designated co-captains each to say a word or two about how they see the forthcoming season. First then, Dale Wheeler, who did such an outstanding job for us last year as our playmaker guard. Dale, what do you say—how do you see things shaping up this year?"

Sitting on the new ball, startled, Dale said, "Well, aah—"

"Stand up, Dale," Coach Burke said.

Dale unfolded himself to his feet, taking the ball into his hands as something upon which to more or less focus. "Well—," he said, glancing away from the ball just briefly, out over the concentration of twenty-five or thirty boys. "Aah, we were city co-champs last year, like Coach Burke said. I did, aah, lots of work myself this summer. Not to be, aah, complacent. Aah, this year means a lot to me. But, aah, if anybody thinks we'll, aah, automatically just win this year, then we'll lose, because that's wrong. Because one thing, the one thing we have to, aah, guard against is being overconfident, and, aah, that's one thing, as co-captain, to say the least, I'm not going to let happen. No way."

"Thank you, Dale, that's pretty well put. Joe, Joe Dillard, what do you have to say? As it turns out, you're not a professional athlete just yet."

The group of boys laughed warmly in response to the coach's remark, happy, it seemed, to be on this certain side of things. Dale was repositioning himself on his ball seat and it was then, after the fact, as Sonny Joe was standing to speak, that he found himself stricken with stage fright. Dale had never spoken to a group in such a way before and, as in other things unknown to him, had been unaware that it had anything to do with him. He had started to tremble. And, sitting on the ball, he realized that unusual sounds were active within his ears in such a way that he hardly heard at all what was being said by Sonny Joe. He sat in awareness of his quaking knees and his living stomach, hands, neck, and face, a fullness of water between his ears. To heck with that stuff, he thought. He was here to play.

Coach Burke was speaking again and the others were all at once getting to their feet. Dale did the same. His thought now was that well, he had done it, that was for sure. He had given his little pep talk and it was something a leader had to do. He had done it and now it was time to do what he was really here to do—put the ball in the hoop.

"Let's go, you guys," he said and clapped his hands as half of them moved with him, the other half with Sonny Joe, lining up on either side to start their opening drill.

In bed that night, in the dark, Dale listened for his father to come home from working the second shift at Chevrolet. He was looking forward—the news seemed a small gift to present—to telling his father that his very own plant supervisor, this huge man named Mr. Von Bothner, had been at his school that afternoon. The man had two sons, he would explain, who wanted to come into the city to go to school and play basketball, just as his own son played basketball, he would imply, his son who was already captain . . . well, co-captain, of his junior high Scholastic League team.

Dale was deeply asleep, however, and his father still had not come home, and later, turning over at some point, barely waking, he knew from a certain absence of sound that the apartment remained empty and that it was too late, too far into the night, to go out and have conversation in the kitchen. There was no telling where his father was or what stage of intoxication, or mood, he might be in by that hour, and to Dale's surprise, an odd feeling of loneliness passed through him in his inability to pass on his small bit of news.

Deeper into the night, perhaps into the morning, Dale awakened to music. His father had made it home; music meant he was half in the bag. Then Dale heard something else, a voice, a woman's voice, he realized, and the small shock of this brought him more fully awake.

He listened. Yes, a woman's voice. Even as the two of them were speaking softly, playing the music softly, it was clear from the pitch of her voice and her giggles—they had to be half bombed, Dale thought—that his father had brought a woman home.

Dale listened less carefully then. Only once before had his father brought a woman home, but it had been long ago, on a Saturday afternoon one summer, and after a brief stay and by unspoken mutual agreement with his father, Dale had left to go downtown to a movie. Now, knowing from the movement of voices that his father's bedroom door was opened, Dale listened even less carefully, then covered his head with his arm and pillow to find his way back into his dream of winning it all.

As day was breaking, Dale awakened once more to the music. It wasn't the volume which reached him, for unless his father was excessively drunk he did not play a record excessively loud. Rather it was the repetition which, as now, usually made its way into his consciousness, the words going around and around until they got into his heart and mind, where they would remain for no less a time than forever:

When I come home at night,
She will be waiting . . .
And she'll be the truest doll
In all the world. . . .

Dale lay there. Shapes were grayly visible, taking on color. The music meant that the woman was still there. Life with his hard-drinking dad. It had almost always been this way, and Dale had no more idea now than ever of how to make his way out through the possible mine field awaiting him in the living room and kitchen.

Than have a fickle-minded,
Real live girl . . .

Washed and dressed, ready for school, Dale opened the hallway door—to an immediate smell of cigarettes, ashes, drinking, the soft music—and entered the living room, trusting and hoping that they were not there, that they were asleep. A single high-heeled shoe was on the floor, and there was another, partially under the couch, and the door to his father's bedroom was several inches ajar. The music played. Other times Dale had turned off the phonograph, had picked up a little and grabbed a bite to eat, but this time, slipping on his jacket, getting his schoolbooks in hand, making no sound, he opened the kitchen door like a burglar and felt relief at once as he stepped outside into the brisk October air.

Down the exposed rear stairway, between houses to the sidewalk, Dale walked along, thinking to get away before he was called back. Then he began to wonder where he might stop to buy himself something for breakfast. Only when he was two or three blocks away did a worrisome thought about his father come to mind. Was he okay? What if something was wrong? Should he have checked to be sure? Was the woman okay? Dale felt a pull to go back, to be sure, but kept walking. Lower Downtown was just ahead; there were twenty-four-hour diners there and buses which would take him to school, and even as the old worrisome crow of his father kept fluttering in the back of his mind, telling him something was wrong and help was needed, Dale continued walking.

In the gym, Dale pushed the wide broom, keeping it angled not to lose any bits of green sweeping compound. He tried to focus his thoughts on what he was doing and not on his father and the woman and whatever problems they might present to him. A binge. It was different, there being a woman with him, but all signs pointed to a binge. Dale pushed the broom. Push-push. Push-push.

What occurred to him, however, as bits of sweeping compound slid away and he reached automatically to recover them, was how little control he had over where his mind chose to go. His mind had a mind of its own. That woman. Some barfly floozie, he imagined. Another drinker. Would she be there after school? Would his father miss work? If he did, that was it, he might miss work for a week. Would he show up here today and drop a bottle on the gymnasium floor? During practice? Would he stagger into Miss Tur-bush's room and offer to give a lecture on love or sing them all a song?

Oh, there had been times when his father had made the other kids laugh. Picking them up downtown after a Sunday matinee, a little juiced only, driving a couple kids home, there had been times when his father had had them giggling and once someone even said to him, "Your dad's a great guy!" Pleased, Dale had smiled and would never forget the boy (Jimmy Callahan) and what he said. Other times, though—at least twice—driving them to the lake and picking them up to drive them home, acting like a race driver, his father had blasted onto the shoulder to miss head-on collisions, and one kid had once wept in terror and run from the car without a word when they pulled up in front of his house.

He had not managed a single word to his father about Mr. Bothner, Dale thought as he removed a ball from the ball bin and began to take his shots. He had not managed a word of that news, or a word either about who was designated co-captain, and a returning starter, too.

There's practice today, Dale reminded himself. That's where his thoughts should be. What was in his mind, though, as he kept taking his shots, was a fantasy he had had already of Mr. Bothner—the great, large man—coming out of his office at the Chevrolet factory and talking to, recognizing his father on the basis of his son's basketball skills. Yes, it was what he had imagined yesterday, he saw now. When the giant-size man had stood to watch them practice, and when he had joined their drill and passed off to them, that's where his thoughts had been. How proud his father would be. It would all start to turn around, just like that. Everything. "I had no idea your son was such a basketball player," Dale imagined the big man saying to his father at work. "What a playmaker guard! What an athlete! I only wish my own sons had half the drive, half the leadership and fight and skill."

Turning it around. Basketball. Work and commitment. Dale Wheeler and his dad, on top of the world.

In homeroom each morning, under a fixed cloth banner embroidered WORD POWER, Miss Turbush wrote two words which were similar in some way but had different meanings. Everyone was "CHALLENGED" to know the words before

going on with the day's classes. Dale liked Miss Turbush—
as he had perceived that the white-haired woman liked
him—and he looked forward each morning to the word
game. There were no quizzes, nor any grades or pressure
of any kind. It was merely a homeroom activity, a game
which in her manner, her declared right to challenge anyone to give a definition, the elderly white-haired teacher
made exciting.

> *Invent/create.*
> *Philosophy/psychology.*
> *Perception/conception.*
> *Profane/profound.*
> *Altar/alter.*

Dale liked the game, just as he liked school, and he
especially liked Miss Turbush. Maybe he loved Miss Turbush in some deep, unacknowledged way. He knew, at least,
that he adored her. He thought of her as his favorite teacher,
and she almost always—in her cleverness and attention to
him, to them all—had his attention.

What he liked about school was doing the work. What
he disliked was not doing the work. He had figured out for
himself in about seventh grade that doing the work was the
key. If he did time in the Reference Room during the day,
and if he did time at the kitchen table at night, there was
a payoff the next day in school. Let there be quizzes, tests,
questions; they made him feel good and were just what he
wanted. They were the payoff.

Civics, with Mrs. Cross, was usually his favorite class,
and Mrs. Cross his next-to-favorite teacher. She was the
school's most popular teacher—more popular than Miss
Turbush, who taught math—and was adored by many students in the way that Dale adored his white-haired mentor.
Mrs. Cross's husband was a U.S. congressman, away most

of the time in Washington (the feeling among her students, however unexpressed, had *him* as the deprived party), and her classes every time were exciting, informative, challenging exercises in which the hour slipped away far too quickly.

Dale also liked English, here in ninth grade with one of the tiny Wrights, Mr. or Mrs., and he liked science, history, and drafting. Math, though, was his subject, perhaps for its exactness, but also, he knew, for the very special payoff it provided of learning the steps—plane and solid geometry, algebra, trigonometry—of following the steps and formulas, the theorems and axioms, of seeing an answer emerge and, upon PROVING, the real payoff in math, seeing an answer emerge and match the first answer! He loved proving the answers.

He disliked school when he had not done the work. A different kind of payoff was provided the next day in school when he wasn't prepared, one in which he hated to be in the classroom, hated sitting there and hearing the teacher talk, hated the person within himself trying to hide. Still, it was often a temptation not to do the work and to go ahead and deal with hating himself and everything else the next day. Some of the girls, like Zona Kaplan, seemed to never even come close to not doing their work, but Dale experienced the temptation often. He usually did the work, and he usually liked school, and he liked Miss Turbush, as he thought of it, "a lot," but he missed being ready often enough to know what it was like at times to dislike the person who sat behind Zona Kaplan in homeroom.

There was Zona's black hair close before him now, and Dale had his work ready this morning even if he was not quite alert to things when Miss Turbush turned from writing the day's two words on the board and said, "Dale Wheeler, how are you this morning? Can you add to our word power today?"

There were the words: *Repute/repose.*

Dale felt stymied at once. Still, he did not feel threatened or embarrassed, for they were feelings Miss Turbush somehow managed to keep out of the game.

"Take your time, Dale, think them out," she said.

She liked him. What a wonder it was to him to be liked by this woman. He did not doubt it for a minute. It was in her eyes, and he was trying now to take her at her word. Take your time, he told himself. Come down from the static in your mind and do as she says. Think.

"Well, repute," he said at last. "I know I've heard people say that. Or I've read it. They say that, aah, someone is reputed to be something."

"Such as?"

"Well—that, aah, someone—is reputed to be rich. Or, well, to be a criminal. Like it means a report or something."

"That's VERY good, Dale—excellent," she said. "Does 'repute' report that something is SO? Or that it's only THOUGHT to be so?"

"Thought to be, I'd say," Dale said, and he knew he was feeling good for the first time today.

"Rep-u-tay-shun," she said. "Do you know that word?"

"Yes."

"Do you see the relationship between REPUTE and REPUTATION? Of course you do. I know you do. What about REPOSE? Does 'repose' mean the same thing?"

"No, the words you put up never mean the same thing," Dale said with a smile, a little daringly.

"Well, I might fool you one of these days," Miss Turbush said. "Although I don't like to play tricks. Games, yes, I like games. But I don't believe in tricks. Have we done 'tricks' and 'games'? Tell me the meaning of 'repose.' "

"Well—repose. Repose?"

"Have you ever heard of someone 'lying in repose'?" she said.

"Oh yes," Dale said. "I've heard that, I've read that."

"To be 'in repose'?"

"Yes," Dale said.

"Fine, then. It's used that way. What does it mean?"

"Well, I think it means to be—resting. Asleep. Maybe even dead."

This drew a laugh.

Miss Turbush said, "No, that's quite good, Dale. Really quite good. 'Repose' can mean any of those, it's true. A person may be CALM. Or TRANQUIL. In repose. AND, it's true, a BODY, a DEAD BODY, may LIE IN REPOSE. No, that's good, Dale. You THINK quite well on your feet and it's something I want you to get to know about yourself, do you hear me?"

Dale looked back at Miss Turbush as she sat down at her desk and turned to do other things. His throat seemed to thicken. An urge was in him to go to the front of the room and touch her. He wanted to stand next to her, and touch her. He wanted to kiss her cheek. He knew, too, that if he looked away just then his eyes would film over more than they had already and someone might notice and say that a teacher had made him cry.

That afternoon the giant man wore the same gray sweatshirt and the same white sneakers—which sneakers Dale had determined to be the actual professional shoes of the Fort Wayne Zollner Pistons—but charcoal pants today, somehow indicating that he had come directly from his job in the office above the long plant beside the river downtown. Did he know by now, Dale wondered, that his father was one of the men who worked on the line below where the new cars were churned out?

Dale worked pointedly hard again, called up all his moves and concentration in an effort to impress the visitor. He drew comments from Coach Burke, from other players. Every time he managed a glance, however, the giant-size figure was at a distance and seeming to look elsewhere.

Only when Coach Burke was working with the centers and forwards at one end did Mr. Bothner move onto the floor to speak and touch a ball. Like others among the guards, Dale paused now and then to look back and watch what was going on. And only once in this time, it seemed, did an image come to mind, and quickly disappear, of his father being bombed, waiting for Dale to come home from school to help him get back on his feet.

The woman? Dale had nearly forgotten her. Would she still be there? What if he let himself into the apartment and found them in a naked pile on the floor?

The giant with silver-gray hair finally demonstrated some moves, and had them all staring in amazement. He was working with Sonny Joe Dillard. Who else, Dale thought. Making some point, pushing out and up into a hook shot, both hands taking the ball high—at the last instant keeping the ball in one hand like it was a volleyball—he returned both feet to the floor to resume talking. Arms and hands extended had made his size all the more apparent, however. New Bob Feller or not, Sonny Joe was like a sapling next to a great oak which, wings spread, was the size of a couple great oaks.

It's what the real pros look like, Dale thought. Bigger than life. The Tiger players he had seen looked like that. Vic Wertz. Frank Lary. George Kell. Art Houtterman. Seen in person they looked twice as big as in their pictures in the papers. Veins, muscles, the size of their heads, noses, eyes, even their teeth—everything was larger than life, and it told, he thought, on why they were the real pros.

He also continued to imagine Mr. Bothner's two sons as awkward, stringbean sissies. And he continued to imagine catching the man's eye, stealing his attention, and having remarks passed on to his father in the plant. Things beginning to turn around. So it was that when the time came for their full-court scrimmage and an opportunity occurred, Dale gave his all and then some to a drive down the center against Hal Doyle and—it worked! hot damn!—hung high, turned in the air, took the block, and put away his double reverse lay-up. He had practiced the shot a thousand, two thousand times or more, and it drew a smile and slap over the hair from Sonny Joe, and someone said to Hal Doyle, "Jock's on the floor, Doyle." But when Dale sneaked his glance to see how he had been seen, the colossal man was no longer there.

Till then . . . till then . . .
My darling, please wait for me . . .
Till then, till I can hold you again. . . .

Dale sang into water streaming down over his head and face. He sang with feeling, if not with happiness. He was the last one in the shower, probably the last one in the locker room, and maybe the last one in the entire school.

He had scrubbed and shampooed excessively, and now he was done singing, too, even as he continued to stand under the flow of water. Only when he was back at his locker, getting dressed, and Slim, the locker room man, passed by and said, "Good Lord, you still here?" did he quite admit to himself how much he was putting off going home. It was the same old routine. The uncertainty. Anything might await him at home.

Out in the air, which always felt so thin after rinsing for an hour or more in the shower, Dale admitted to himself that he had to go home, if only to check. It was a walk of about a mile, though, and he kept taking his time, trying not to think of anything. He looked to the gutter in search of lost treasure as he walked along. In first grade again.

At last he turned onto Chevrolet Avenue, and the house was there. Its top—their small apartment with its slanted ceilings—had not burned down. Things hadn't gone that far. Not yet at least.

Dale looked around for his father's car. The presence of the green Chevy, when his father should have been at work, was always a giveaway sign. There at the wrong time, it meant his father had missed work and was probably drinking and in an unpredictable mood. In an early stage, he might be in thrall to something emotional and sentimental, intoxicating in itself, coming from Hank Williams, or Kitty Wells, or old Jimmie Rodgers, going around and around on the phonograph. Or he might be in a mood to give speeches and tell stories Dale had no wish to hear.

Or, as it had also happened, although not recently, his father might be fun to be with, might have Dale shedding tears of laughter at his jokes and stories, as they went out for fish and chips or, in summer, drove to the lake to wade and swim and play in the cool, green water.

No car. Dale looked carefully. The car wasn't there. And it was only as he was sitting at the kitchen table eating Franco American spaghetti—directly from the saucepan, where he had cross-cut the orange-and-white mess half a dozen times—that he wondered if the woman might have been a good influence and had gotten his father to get himself together and to work on time. It was the first time Dale had considered that a certain woman might be just the thing.

City League. As Dale put away the last spoonful of Franco American, he was thinking that tomorrow, as early as tomorrow, he would get together with Sonny Joe and confirm the team they would enter this year. Ten players, Dale thought. No more than ten. And, at last, he'd reveal to Joe the name he had in mind. It had been next to impossible keeping it to himself this long, but he had pulled it off. The Blue Arrows. He still liked it, he thought. But as the time was so near, so were his doubts near the surface again. Retrieving his notebook, he opened to a clean page, printed across the top:

THE BLUE ARROWS

Yes, he liked it. The name was cool, no doubt about it. Putting things together now, he thought. This was the time to do it. Two, two and a half weeks ahead of time. It would show yet again that leadership was something he happened to have in his pocket. Initiative. He had those things. He had them, he thought, because he knew he had them. He thought of things. He did not wait to be told, and it made him someone who did the telling. It was why he was a captain. It was why he was asked to give a pep talk to other players. He thought of things.

What actually went on in the heads of others? he asked himself. Clothes and reputations? Girls? To grow a duck's tail or not and the question of white bucks versus blue suede shoes?

His mind kept running ahead, too, to the finale to come at season's end. The City Auditorium, downtown, where he had yet to put up a single shot. Two or three thousand people showed up for the finals, including the city high school coaches doing their scouting and, as always, of course, it would be ten times as exciting as anything that ever happened in Scholastic League. Yet again, he could hardly wait. They had only to guard against overconfidence, he reminded himself. As he had warned them all. And as long as he had his say, it was what they'd do. To say the least. Looking close then, he entered his hopes and dreams for the year into his notebook:

Win the City.
Be co-captain.
Drive a car.
Do it with a girl.
Do it with Zona Kaplan as the girl.
Turn it all around.

He sang out, "Take my hand . . . I'm a stranger in paradise. . . ." And for lack of anything else to do, he took up the *Official Rule Book* Coach Burke had given to him as co-captain and began to read it through again. A thin booklet, twenty-seven pages of small print. Well, he'd be ready, he thought. Refs wouldn't catch him off guard. No way. Not as a captain who thought of things.

"Oh, lost in a wonderland . . . ," he sang as he took in the small print.

Into Dale's depth of sleep that night—early, his body told him—there came a *knuk-knuk*. And another.

A voice was speaking to him. It was the old pattern. He perceived the silhouette in the doorway, and into his woolly sleep, knew what it was. Home from work, on the sober side of things tonight, his father was there to apologize.

". . . said I have some Coneys. You hungry, Redsie? Come on and have a Coney."

It was early, when his sleep was deepest, and Dale was still waking up. Still, he managed to sleep-moan "Uhh," of a language, he knew, his father understood to mean he was coming out.

"Good," his father said. "Good—something I want to tell you."

Barefooted, in his underwear, eyes squinting, Dale made his way into the lighted space. He was still twenty or thirty percent asleep. Two hot dogs, removed from the sack, were on top of the sack on the table, wrapped separately as always in heavy sheets of waxed paper. Coney Island dogs were always good in the middle of the night, and tonight they would be the best, more satisfying to his taste mechanism even than the last time. It was always this way; it seemed to be something his father knew in serving them up at such an hour. Coney Islands coming in on the dreamland express. Warm doughnuts, too. Just like the girls of his dreams, they were more exotic, more sensual and satisfying than any he had ever known in daylight.

"Help yourself," he heard his father say.

Dale folded back the waxed paper. There was the secret-recipe chili sauce topped with chopped white onion, all smothering the natural-casing dog as heavy as lead pipe, for Coney Islands of memory weighed not ounces but pounds.

Dale stretched his mouth so wide it hurt, managed to push in and chop off a small meal. Food. He chomped, chewed, salivated, put it away. Eating brought him around; his eyes were adjusting to the light. There was his father, smiling, pleased, home again after yesterday's excursion into a sea of Seagram's 7.

"Partner, listen, sorry about this morning. You know? That old gal . . . well, I don't know . . . she's a pretty good old soul . . . anyway, whatever I said . . . did I say things to you? Anyway, you gotta realize it ain't your old dad talking to you at a time like that. What it is, it's an old snake that hides in the bottom of a whiskey bottle waiting to sneak up on him. Forgive me, will you."

Dale hardly gestured, to indicate that it was in the past. He drank from a glass of milk his father had poured.

"How're things in school?" his father said.

Dale gestured faintly again, to say things were okay.

"Tell you, son, I know I've got to do something to shake the old jug and the grip it has on me. I've been giving it a lot of thought. Thought about it all day. One thing I know is, I can't do it without your help. You and nobody else. Know what I'm saying? I been thinking of trying this AA outfit. They meet there by the plant. I mean I don't think I'm that far gone, not yet at least, but maybe they know something I don't. What I do know is if you're on my side, you know, then I might be able to do it. What do you say?"

Dale had paused between bites, and he looked at his father. AA had never been mentioned, although his father had appealed to him for help—under the influence—many times before. Dale had learned in time that it was a line, but he always said he'd help. Now he said, "What do you want me to do?"

"Be on my side," his father said. "That's the main thing. Don't be against me."

Dale nodded. He took another bite. He knew already that it was only another line.

"Will you?" his father said.

"Sure."

"That's good—that's good to hear," his father said.

AA was new, though, and Dale tried again to believe. He had tried other times to believe, but no promises had ever been kept.

"What if you went on first shift?" Dale said, thinking he would at least suggest something.

"Well, it pays a lot better on second," his father said.

Dale nodded and let it go. Then he said, "Mr. Von Bothner has been coming to basketball practice, at my school."

"The big shot from the plant?" his father said. "That's who you mean?"

"He comes to basketball practice."

"Why's he doing that? He's a big old bird, for sure; maybe he played some basketball in his time."

"Oh, he was a big star is what the coach said. His sons—

what it is, is he has two sons who want to come into town, to go to my school and play basketball, and he's checking out the competition or something."

"They any good?"

"Oh, I don't know; nobody's seen them. I bet I'm better, though."

"Well, I bet you are," his father said, smiling. "He may be a big shot at Chevrolet Plant Four—but in life, on the field of battle, we'll show the bastards, won't we."

He hadn't meant to brag or make a joke, Dale thought. Rather, it had been a sudden word from the heart, here in the heart of the night. "They live on a horse farm in Fenton Meadows," Dale said. "Both his sons, they both won the Soap Box Derby and went to the nationals at Akron. Now they want to come into the city to play basketball."

"Well, sounds like they got a lot—but I still bet you can show them a thing or two. In fact, this year, I'll tell you what—this year I'm going to get back to see one of these games of yours. I am, I swear. Would it make you nervous? Your old dad slipping in to watch? I'll be on my best behavior, I can tell you that."

"Sounds fine," Dale said, even as the idea did make him feel nervous.

"That's what I'm going to do," his father said. "I am. And I'll tell you what I'm going to do right now. Haven't joined that AA outfit quite yet, you know. Going to have just a little nip here. Rome, you know, wasn't built in a day."

Dale nodded, knew it was time to withdraw, to return to bed. "Well, thanks for the Coney," he said.

"Sleep tight now, son. Let me know, so I can come to one of those games of yours."

Dale nodded, continued into the unlighted side of the apartment.

Lying in the dark, Dale realized that the sleepiness which

had so filled him was gone now. He lay gazing into darkness, tried to call up a shot at the buzzer, a driving lay-up, something to take him under. At last he found it, but it wasn't a game this time as much as the details of arriving at the City Auditorium, using a locker room he imagined to be spacious and plush, going out onto the floor before two or three thousand people, one of them his father, who would be more proud of his son than he had ever been of anything in his life. Winning the City—it was like a stream of warm water, and Dale slipped back into it and floated off once more into the heart of the night.

"We already got a team," Sonny Joe said.

Dale did not understand. The light was poor in the annex hallway near Metal Shop, and for the moment no one else was around. He had just run into Joe Dillard, had just remarked that it was time to set up a meeting, time to get their team roster together for City League.

"Who has a team?" Dale said. "What do you mean?"

"What I said," Joe said. "We have a team. And a sponsor. Coach is going to let us practice in the gym."

"Who does?" Dale said, still confused, even as awareness—a shape in the leaves one had thought was a branch is seen to have markings, is thick, coiled, alive—was coming through to him. His heart was shocked and may have known ahead of his mind. He heard himself say, as Joe had not responded, "No one said anything to me about it. Since when?"

"You're not on it," Joe said.

"Since when?" Dale said again, and his words were still off-key and awful, even to himself. "What's that mean?"

"Mr. Bothner put a team together. We met at their house last night. We have a sponsor already, everything's all set."

"Last night—? I don't get it. At their house?"

"Hey, Wheels, don't blame it on me," Joe said. "We had a team meeting at their house. With our fathers."

"Who did? No one told me about it."

"That's because you're not on it. Didn't you hear what I said? Didn't nobody tell you?"

"I'm not on it—? What's that mean?"

"I don't know why they didn't ask you," Joe said. "But they didn't." He made an expression and stood looking down, the faintest impatience on his face at Dale's ignorance.

"What sponsor?" Dale said. "I just don't get it."

"Look," Joe said, and he raised the palm of one hand. "Don't take it out on me. I didn't put it together."

"Who's taking anything out on you? What sponsor? I just don't get it is all."

"Michigan Truckers," Joe said. "It's a company Mr. Bothner owns or something, I don't know. Or he's on the board or something. Hey, I have to go."

"Who else is on it?" Dale said in what sounded like another person's voice. He had tried to sound reasonable, but his voice was not his anymore. The message from Joe was a rifle shot, that's what he knew. It was a rifle shot and it was on its way to his heart and he could not believe it even as he knew it could not be stopped.

"Look, don't blame me," Joe said. "It sure wasn't my idea."

"I didn't say it was," Dale said, and he was taking steps after the lanky boy as he moved away. "I just don't know what you're talking about," he said. His eyes were glazed, Dale knew, and he knew that the rifle shot was still on its way, was moving toward him with certainty and was going to strike him.

"I gotta go," Joe said. He made an expression, an angling of his face, and moved away.

Dale stopped and stood there, looked to the empty hallway. He did not know where was he going. He had a class
to attend, he knew, but for the moment he did not know
which class or in which direction he had been headed.
Perhaps other students had passed as he and Joe had talked,
he wasn't sure. He wasn't going to cry, was he? Why would
he do that, when nothing made sense and he didn't even
know what was going on?

Had classes started? Given the emptiness of the hallway,
he knew they had, although he could not recall the ringing
of second bell.

It passed through him again—what Joe had said. Then
he didn't believe it. It couldn't be. It had to be a dream.
He was in the middle of a dream. Or it was some kind of
joke he had walked into.

He was walking along the school's rarely used annex
corridor, which passed Metal Shop. He could see that. The
corridor was real. And no one was peeking around a corner
giggling. Wasn't he here? He looked to the mesh-wire glass
in the Metal Shop door. It was painted a lime color on the
inside, casting a faint green tone over the space. He looked
to the green-tinted light, thought to try to touch the light
to see it melt or fold or something and prove that all of this
was a strange dream.

He walked down the corridor. He had a class to get to.
It was what he had to do. Get to class. He walked on, even
as he knew all over again that the bullet was on its way still
and in time was going to arrive and strike him. He was
aware of this, even as the awareness seemed to belong to
another.

Michigan Truckers. He had been impressed with the
name at once. *Michigan Truckers.* It was the coolest name
he had ever heard, he thought, while other things Joe had
said jumped around in his mind too rapidly to fit together.
They had put together a team and he wasn't on the team?

Dale was near his classroom—wasn't this where he was supposed to be, Mr. Wright's English class?—and the information kept jumping around in his mind and he could not escape or put in its place that this bullet was after him still and he could not get away from it. Oh, none of this can be, he said to himself then, because he was good and everybody knew he was good. They wouldn't do this to him. Not to him. Had he been too proud—too cocky? Was that what it was? Was it because they were poor? Because his father drank and could not be included as one of the fathers to go to somebody's house?

In his classroom, Dale became aware of himself again, sitting and staring out the window. There was the sky and, across the street—he studied them as if he had never seen them before—pencil lines of telephone wires. It came over him again in a wave—his throat and stomach seeming to fill—that he had been left off the team of which he had dreamed a thousand dreams, and as he felt his heart flutter and his throat began to fill, he wondered if the bullet was entering him now, was starting to penetrate its target.

He looked to sky and wires through filmed eyes and knew that he was breaking down and that he had to take off. An intake of breath, a gasp, got out. He had nearly cried. He sat trying to hold the fullness within and it called up wetting his pants at age five when something began to warm his pants all on its own and was beyond control and everyone was going to see the big wet spot and know what it was.

He got to his feet and circled the rear of the room toward the door. He had no idea what was going on in class. "Dale—?" Mr. Wright said.

He entered the empty hallway, continued walking. Miss Turbush's room was along this corridor, too, and a thought was in his mind to go to her, to cry to her to help him. If he spoke to Miss Turbush, though, he knew he might collapse, he might even fall clinging to the frail, elderly woman, might grip her legs and cry out to her to help him. He hesitated in his walking, was tempted, because he knew that Miss Turbush was one person who could go to Coach Burke and to Mr. Von Bothner, too, and tell them they could not do this to this young man, because he was a young man who could think on his feet and they had better get themselves busy and undo what they had done to him, and they had better do it in a hurry, too, or she was going to swat their knuckles with a ruler and make them stay after school and clean blackboards and erasers for the rest of their lives.

Dale did not turn back. He continued hard on his way to the main door, wanting to make it outside before he lost control. He began to run, or jog, like a child running to the bathroom even as it may have been too late already and the child's pants were too wet for anything to make a difference.

In the air, Dale walked, gasping in spasms, walked and loped, until he was across the street which passed before the school and was walking hard down a residential side street, leaving the school behind, and still he did not break down entirely and cry. He was unable nonetheless to get away from the awful feeling, to leave behind any of the hurt which had him in its squeeze. If only he could cry and cry and have it done with and out of him as in some long-ago child-time shocking hurt like the death of his cat, Ginger.

No chance. It was too twisted and strange and he knew it wouldn't go away. Nor did he know where to go. The bullet was in his heart, he knew that. He had been hit back there somewhere and now his heart was torn and no matter where he ran to, or where he tried to hide, he would not be able to be away from the torn hole which would stay with him. They had hit him like a bull's-eye, right in his dream. Was it because he was poor and had been too cocky? he wondered. Was it because his father couldn't go with the other fathers because he was an alcoholic and a factory worker and a hillbilly from Arkansas while they all lived in houses and went to church and had mothers at home and Sunday dinners? Was it because . . . because he had thought he could turn everything around?

He walked on the residential sidewalk, trying not to cry and then not being able to hold it back entirely and gasping madly as his eyes filled. In this span of time he was barely in control of himself and in some moments was not at all in control. Later he would recall going onto the porch of a house with green shingles and rapping on a screen door, not quite knowing at the time that he was doing it or why, maybe to appeal to someone to help him, or to call his father, although if he was seen from within the green house, no one came to the door.

Had his thought really been to call his father? It seemed, after the fact, to be what he had in mind—to ask someone to call his father, to say it was Dale and that it had turned out that he couldn't turn things around and he was the one who needed help now.

He slipped in and crouched behind shrubs at the side of another house, hid like a child heartsick and angry with everything. Hiding there, he pinched and tore leaves and small branches and threw them down and continued to gasp in spurts. He thought of getting his father and having him come back to beat them up and make them sorry, to make them let him be on the team, even as he knew within that none of this could possibly be.

He recalled the time that Mr. Dusoe had picked on him, had held him down, and he had gone home to get his father, and for a moment at least, there in the dirt and pebbles, in the chilled air, wadding leaves and twigs, he seemed to believe there was something he and his father could do and how sorry they'd all be. He was fighting Jimmy Dusoe and was beating him up and Mr. Dusoe grabbed

him from behind and held him and let Jimmy hit him half
a dozen times, and when he jerked and kicked free from
being held he said it had been a fair fight and it wasn't fair
to hold him like that and he had better watch out because
he was going home to get his father. And when his father
asked him how big this guy was—Mr. Dusoe was a tall
string bean of a man, inches taller than his father—he said
to his father that he didn't know, and his father tossed off
a drink, and winked at him, and said, "Okay, Redsie, I
guess we better go show that sonofabitch what we're made
of," and Dale had never been more proud in his life than
when he and his father left and walked back down the street,
and up onto Dusoe's porch, where Mr. Dusoe's tub of a
wife stood behind him where he stood behind his locked
screen door and she kept bellowing at him although he was
no more than an inch away, "Don't you go out there,
George," as if George would have gone out in a hundred
years, Dale thought, and his father told the trembling man
at last that he did not appreciate his putting a hand on his
son and it was something he was never to do again, or he'd
have to have a hell of a lot more than a screen door to
protect him.

Cheeks feeling sunburned from dried tears, Dale became
aware of himself, walking down the street toward school.
Maybe thirty or forty minutes had passed since he had gone
by in the other direction, but now he had an idea of what
he could do. Coach Burke. Yes, he thought, Coach Burke.
It isn't fair, he heard himself telling the man. It isn't fair,
because the City League team is always made up of kids
from their school and it isn't fair to not let him be on the
team. How could they do that? It didn't make sense!
    Coach Burke, he kept thinking and hoping against hope.

Coach Burke was in charge and he wouldn't stand for it. Would he?

Everybody knew he was one of the best players, he heard himself telling the man. Everybody knew that.

Entering the building, though, he felt such dread and confusion within that he wasn't sure, the closer he came to actually speaking to the coach, what line of appeal or reasoning he might try. He was afraid, too, all at once, that putting himself up as captain as he had, if only in his thoughts, would be added evidence to tip the scales against him. "They had thought to reconsider," the Sportscaster in the sky would say, "but in the light of still more false representations being made by this young man . . ."

Please let it all not be, Dale thought as he walked through the locker room on his way to Coach Burke's office. He'd do anything to have it all not be. Let it be some joke by Joe Dillard, he thought. Let it be that. He wouldn't even be mad at him for playing a joke on him like that.

Still uncertain what he would say, he tapped on Coach Burke's office door there in the tunnel. Yes, he knew he shouldn't be here, he knew that. He should be in class and this was something he should bring up later and through the right channels. He knew that. But—it's so unfair of Mr. Bothner, he heard himself saying to Coach Burke. It's so unfair. It doesn't make sense.

No one answered. He tapped again and, against his better judgment, tried the knob, but as the wooden door opened and he looked in, the office was dim and empty.

Looking into the boy's gym, seeing Coach Burke at one end, whistle swaying from his neck as he directed rows of seventh-grade boys in an exercise, Dale knew again that he should not interrupt like this in the middle of a class. Still, it was an emergency and he was a leader, and there he was, walking over the gym floor in his street shoes, going around to where the man, in slacks and sweatshirt, had his arms extended skyward like an official signaling a touchdown. "What is this—what do you want?" Coach Burke said, keeping his arms up as he looked at Dale.

"They left me off the team or something," Dale said. "I don't know."

"What are you doing here?" the man said. "Shouldn't you be in class?"

Something sank in Dale; he knew that all was lost. "It's not fair," he said. "It doesn't make sense."

"I don't like this," Coach Burke said. "You should be in class." Hands at his sides, he was looking directly now into Dale's eyes.

"It just isn't fair," Dale said again. "They left me off the team. Mr. Bothner did. I didn't do anything."

Knowing he was losing a struggle as his eyes blurred again and not even caring that it was in front of thirty or forty seventh graders, Dale heard the coach call "Free time" and felt the man's sudden grip-push of his elbow as he turned toward the office. "Come with me!" the man hissed at him. "You get a hold of yourself—right now—do you hear me?!"

They walked along, the man pushing his elbow. "I do not appreciate being interrupted in the middle of a class— not one iota!" the coach said at his side. Iota. Whenever the man used that word, Dale knew he was somehow lying or just trying to confuse things.

Coach Burke opened his office door.

As he was pushed in, Dale pulled his elbow away from being touched—he just did not like being pushed at that moment—and was within a heartbeat, he knew, of turning on the man in some out-of-control way, perhaps to try to hurt him.

The coach slammed the door, glared at him. "Act tough with me, young man," he said, "and you won't be on any team in this school ever again!"

Dale knew his defeat was final; it was over. "Why are

you mad at me?" he said to the man. "I haven't done anything. This is my third year playing here and nobody has played harder. And you know that. And now you act like you're mad at me and I haven't done anything."

Don't cry, Dale was saying to himself, even as his eyes were filling again. "You—," he said to the man, who only watched him as if from a detached perspective. "You act mad at me and I haven't done anything."

The coach still watched him. Dale knew he was going to be different then, and so he was. "Dale," the man said. "Why don't you take it easy for a minute—can you do that?"

"Joe said," Dale said. "Joe Dillard said they were using the gym. Why can't I be on the team? Do they think I'm not good enough or something? I don't get it."

"Dale, hold on now. Just hold on, okay? I'm going to tell you just exactly what it is. Do you hear me? I'm going to tell you just what it is that has happened here. Then I want you to go on to your class and get a hold of yourself. Will you do that? If I explain to you exactly what it is— I'm going to tell you the God's truth, too. If I do that, will you get a hold of yourself and go on to your class? Will you? Yes or no, Dale?"

Dale looked at him, did not reply.

"Look. Dale. I'm saying that I will tell you just what the situation is. You should be flattered is what you should be. Do you hear what I'm saying? Do you HEAR what I'm saying? You should be flattered. But I'm not going to tell you anything until you tell me that you hear what I'm saying and that you will get yourself together and go on to your class. Now—can I tell you what has happened or not? Can I, or not, Dale? I want you to answer me!"

"Yes!" Dale said then.

"These things happen. You understand? They happen like this, and they'll happen at other times in your life too.

They've happened to me, just like they happen to everybody, believe me. Do you hear what I'm saying? Do you?!"

"Yes!" Dale said. "Yes!"

"Dale. Listen. It's not that you're not good enough. That's not what it is at all. What it is—and this is just between the two of us. You're a little too good is what it is. You understand what I'm saying?"

"What does that mean?!" Dale said.

"Dale, listen to me. The man can't have you on his team, or his own son would have to sit on the bench all year. You see what I'm saying? He couldn't put you on the bench, because everyone would know that that wouldn't make sense. What he wants is a team for his two sons to play on. Together. You can't blame him for that, can you? You see, the older boy, he can do okay, because he's quite big and he's learning fast. But the younger boy wouldn't get to play if you were there, and what his father wants to do is to train him to do what you do, which is to be the playmaker guard. You see? Teams are often put together like that. It happens all the time. How can he do that if you're there? You see what I'm saying? You see why I said you should be flattered?"

"That doesn't make it fair," Dale said. "What team am I supposed to be on?"

"Hey, listen to me now. I told you the truth. I said that's what I would do, and I did. Because you have played well for me, it's true, and I've always liked you. You did agree, though—if I told you the truth—you did agree, Dale, that you'd get yourself together and go on to your class. Didn't you agree to that? Didn't you? Dale—did you agree to that or not? I'd like an answer, please! Yes or no? *Did you—*"

"Yes!"

"Fine, then. Fine. Let's get on with things then. Dale, these things happen. Believe me. They always have and they always will. And there is not one tooting thing I can do about a City League team in any case, as you well know, so let's be realistic here. My advice to you is to be happy you've learned a little lesson like this at this point in your life instead of later. You can always sign up with some other team. Mr. Bothner after all has come in here with a sponsor and uniforms and a whole program and he surely gets to have some choice, I would think, about who he wants on his team. If you have a complaint, it's really with him, in any case, not with me, as you well know."

The man was directing him to the door, refraining this time from touching him, and disliking him now, Dale knew, in the same way that he had once liked him.

Ushered to the doorway, Dale managed to say, weakly, "That doesn't make it fair."

There was only eyes-raised impatience from the man, upon the closing of the door.

Dale stood there, the door eight or ten inches from his face. In a glimpse then, as if he had forgotten, he thought he saw who he was. How could he have so completely forgotten something like that? He paused, not knowing what to do next. Should he go on his way or knock once more on the door? Should he bang on the door and cry out? Or should he just walk away? Did he have any choice? What had happened?

Dale felt numb for a moment, walking into the empty locker room. Aftershocks of hurt might return to startle his heart forever, but for the moment he felt only numbness. If anyone saw him walking here, they would probably identify him as an ordinary student, although one who might be truant, skipping gym class, standing in the boys' locker room and not knowing what to do with himself.

He wandered into the empty shower room and stood next to the tile wall between nozzles. The hurt came up in him again. He leaned to the wall there and tried to keep his chest and stomach from trembling. Then it was himself he wanted to be away from, as if he could see why it was that he had been left off the team. For an instant he despised himself. Him and his father. Two of a kind. What fools.

The floor was dry and filmy underfoot. He gazed at the soap-stained trough along the wall and thought how he had been an idiot to have forgotten who he was. The perception seemed to amaze him. How could he have forgotten something like that? He had just gone along like he was one of them, with their trips to Mackinac Island and their Sunday School classes, and they had picked this time to let him know that he wasn't one of them at all. How could anyone be so blind? That's what he wanted to know. How could anyone be so blind they forgot who they were, especially a person who went around thinking he was a leader, and thinking he was a person who thought of things? How could anyone be so blind?

PART
TWO

A voice was coming in upon his jungle of dreams, looking for a place to land. He did not know for a moment if the voice was speaking within his mind or without. "Redsie," he heard it say, and saw a silhouette and began putting it together.

"Redsie, you awake?" his father said, to awaken him.

Coming to the surface, he knew from his father's voice that he was either sober or in a sober mood. Two days had passed since Dale had taken the rifle shot in his heart, and even as he had told himself by now to let it go, he welcomed a chance to say something about it, there in the kitchen, welcomed a chance to try to explain it to someone who would be on his side. Only then did he take in what his father was saying.

"Redsie, we're moving to a new place—tomorrow."

"We're doing what?"

"Moving on, son. Tomorrow and Sunday. Got lots to do."

"When'd this happen?" Dale said, rising to an elbow. "Moving where?"

"Come on and have one of these cinnamon doughnuts and I'll tell you about it. Come on, before they get cold. There's no school tomorrow. We got lots to do."

Had they been asked to move? The music his father played at all hours? His drinking? That woman? It would not be the first time, and whatever might have happened, Dale knew, it would not come out until later. Or never.

In the kitchen, Dale put away one warm doughnut, and another, with glugs of cold milk—he had eaten little in recent days—while his father described their destination. It's a small house, he told him, on the east side, the Civic Park school district.

"Why didn't you tell me?" Dale said.

"Oh, I didn't want you to worry," his father said. "Besides, it just sorta happened quicklike."

"What did?"

"Came time to move on, you know."

"Everything's okay?"

"Nothing to worry about. Everything's fine. We just have lots to do and I need to know that you can help pack and load up tomorrow and Sunday."

"What about school? That's in another district?"

"I figured we'd just let that ride for now. You'll be going to high school next fall—you take the bus over to Whittier for now, I don't think anybody'll have to know the difference. And we'll have the same phone number, so that won't be a problem."

"That's a long bus ride every day."

"Won't be so bad. You take one bus downtown and transfer to another. It's not that far. Have another doughnut. You seem hungry to me; you been eating okay?"

"Yeah."

"Son, it'll be okay. You just have this part of a year left, and where we're going is a lot closer to Central High than if we stayed here. Just kind of take my word for it. I need you to be with me on this, you know. Hear what I'm saying, Curlytop? We're a little behind the eight ball here—can you just take my word for it?"

"I guess so."

"You won't let me down, will you, son? When I need you?"

"No," Dale said.

"Well, there's something else I want to say," his father said.

Awareness came up in Dale of how sober and lucid his father was. He usually turned over new leaves when his eyes were swimming, when his face was covered with stubble and his neck was made of rubber.

"AA," his father said. "That group I told you about. Gets together at Chevy Corners. The anonymous part is you just go by your first name, you see, so nobody has to know who you are. I'm going to give it a try is what I've been thinking. I tell ya something, son. It's gotten so the old jug is like a noose around my neck most of the time. And when I've had a few I feel like such a helpless, broken-down sonofabitch. I just don't like it, and I been thinking, well, maybe it's the only chance I got. I'm not so old I don't have a couple years left is what I figure. And I thought, well, I'd like to see my boy grow up a little more, and have a better life than his old man ever had. That's what I been thinking. Son, there's no reason your life can't be an improvement over mine. I mean that. I was given pretty good chances but I've managed to throw about all of them away. Gone with the wind. What I can do, I been thinking, is help you along so maybe you can do a little better than I ever did my own-damn-self."

Dale did not know what to say. His own confused crisis was there within him, as real as a living creature pacing back and forth.

"Anyway, enough of that for now," his father said. "We're moving—we're going to have a fresh start. Have another one of those doughnuts, why don't you—they're fresh, too."

Dale shook his head no thanks to another doughnut, and had no urge to smile in response to his father's smile. The space that had opened in him to hunger was so filled now that he thought he might be sick to his stomach. Or that he might break down and start gasping again, as he had more than once in the past two days.

Nor was he about to mention Mr. Bothner. He could imagine his father getting angry and reaching for a bottle if he tried to explain what had happened and how destroyed he was. And as his father drank, Dale imagined, he would only grow more angry. What he might do then, Dale knew, was anyone's guess. He might telephone Mr. Bothner, even if it was two o'clock in the morning. He'd telephone and ask for him and he'd be more or less courteous as he built up to telling him what he thought of what he had done. And as much as Dale wanted Mr. Bothner told—even as in a glimmer he entertained a thought of everything being made right again—he knew better. No one was going to say oh, that was just a mistake, we're so sorry, let us undo this and make it right. He just wasn't one of them, with their birthday parties and Sunday dinners, and he never had been. And if his father went too far with Mr. Bothner, or with Mr. Burke, and Dale knew how capable his father was of going too far, he'd have to transfer to another school for sure, because he'd be too ashamed to return to Whittier Junior High.

Wasn't he already? Dale thought. You got destroyed, and you felt so ashamed you thought there were things you'd never be able to do again, people you'd never be able to face, and then you went and did those things and faced those people anyway. You had to. You felt like you were made of crap, for sure, as he had felt in school the last couple days, but he went and did those things anyway. It was how he had felt every step he had taken for two days now, in classrooms, in the hallways, entering and leaving. But there he was. He had walked along, had avoided looking at people, had felt like he couldn't stand up to a flea. But he was there. What else could he do?

What Dale also thought, as he returned to bed and lay awake in the dark, was that his father wasn't so bad. There he was—he was trying again to get himself together. All that booze. Maybe it really was hard to shake it. It sure seemed that way. He loved his father, he thought. He had never quite thought that he loved his father, but as he lay there in the dark, the thought came to him. His eyes were going soft again. His eyes were going soft like that all the time now and he wished they would stop it. He wondered, too, if he loved his father because he was so destroyed now himself and didn't have anything or anyone else to turn to.

Oh, he loved him, Dale thought. He did. He just hadn't thought of it like that. He always liked to see him. At least he always used to. He used to really like to come home and find him there. When he was younger, it was always fun when his father woke him and had him come out to the kitchen to eat and talk. They had some good times. Except recently. Just the last couple years. That was all. The last couple years.

He liked listening to his father tell stories, too, Dale thought. There had been times when he was so funny it had made his eyes fill with tears and his stomach hurt from laughing. And lots of his stories were really interesting, too. It was just when he was sloppy drunk that it was a problem. If it weren't for times like that he'd be great, Dale thought. He'd be just as big a deal as Mr. Von Bothner, and he'd sure be a bigger deal than stupid Burkebutt.

His father wouldn't be a cheater, that was for sure. Just because he drank didn't mean he'd be a cheater. In fact, maybe he drank, Dale thought, because he *wasn't* a cheater.

One thing he knew for sure: His father would never do to anyone what Coach Burke and Mr. Bothner had done to him. Not in a hundred years. Not in a thousand. They could bribe and torture him and he wouldn't do that. His father would die first. Because he just wasn't like that. It was more than those Bothner kids could ever say about their dad. Maybe his father was only a factory worker, Dale thought, as his emotions were overtaking him again. And maybe he got lost in a bottle sometimes. But he would never cheat on a fifteen-year-old kid like they did, because he wasn't a dirty cheater and liar like that. He wasn't, Dale thought. Those dirty cheater bastards! *Liars!* he thought, seeing it as the worst possible thing to be. *You liars!*

Before anything was packed in the morning, Dale knew that the creature within him was on its way out. Maybe it had been on its way out all along. He did not know if he thought his father could do something about it, only that the mad creature was close by and that he had little sense of anything else, no discipline or perspective, it seemed, had nothing within him besides the confused pacing monster of hurt and anger.

He picked at the edge of the scrambled eggs and toast his father cooked and served. "Guess you had too many doughnuts during the night," his father said.

Dale held his problem just under the surface. Sitting at the table, his father remarked that it was the last time they'd ever have breakfast on Chevrolet Avenue and what they'd do in the morning was go downtown to a diner, maybe drive out to a truck stop on Dort Highway.

Dale tried another pea-size bite, pushed it toward his unaccommodating stomach. If his father was nipping swigs, Dale had not seen him and had not noticed any telltale odor. It's the move, Dale thought. He's going easy because of the move. Moves had never made him go easy before, however, and Dale wondered if his father might really be serious about AA. It was hard to believe. What would things be like if his father stayed sober? As Dale tried to consider the question, the monster kept pushing toward the surface, threatening to make him sick again.

On a drive to Kroger's, to pick up whatever cardboard boxes they could find, Dale started to let it out. "Pop," he said, and it was there on his lips just as his father said "Watch it!" to the windshield and braked before a new Bel Air pulling in front of them. It was like a moment in a movie, and Dale wondered if it was another sign to him to keep his troubles to himself.

Back in the kitchen his father was sorting boxes, putting one, then another aside for Dale to take to his bedroom. Dale put boxes inside boxes and all at once the monster was in his throat. "Pop," he said. "I got really screwed at school—in City League—I was really screwed by Mr. Bothner, who is a dirty cheater, I don't care what he is at the plant . . . ," and in the midst of his gasping, his story cascaded forth.

His father heard him to the end. He stood looking to the linoleum, nodding some as Dale made his case in a rush of emotion. Dale said, for the third or fourth time, "Even Coach Burke said it was because I was better than his younger son . . . ," and trailed off, feeling an aftertaste of shame.

His father was looking at him. He reached an arm to him and pulled him to his side. "Jesus, that sounds like one of the dirtiest tricks I ever heard," he said. "To steal away something from a boy who has worked so hard for it. He should be ashamed of himself."

"It is like stealing—isn't it?" Dale said.

They stood in silence and Dale knew that something was different. His father was sober. There would be no phone calls, no challenges to Mr. Bothner to have it out in the street. Did his father believe he was as good a player as he said he was? Maybe he no longer believed it himself. Still, what his father said next surprised him. "Son—I'm afraid what we have to do right now is get our stuff together and get moved to our new place. That's what we have to do right now. You know what I mean?"

"Oh, sure," Dale said. He nodded and was having difficulty making eye contact with his father. "I didn't mean— I mean I just wanted—I don't know."

"We'll see later if there's anything we can do about Mr. Von Bothner," his father said.

"Sure," Dale said. "I didn't mean—you know."

"I've got one too many things on my mind right now. I don't mean to turn my back on this problem of yours, because it sure doesn't sound fair. It's just that—"

"It's okay," Dale said. "It's okay. I know we have all this stuff to do. I only wanted—I don't know—it's okay."

"We'll come back to it," his father said.

Dale nodded in agreement.

On a glance, seeing that his father was going to offer a reassuring wink, Dale reached for the two boxes and carried them away. Everything had backfired, he saw, as he put the boxes down in his bedroom. His dream of turning things around, of leading them into the future. What a joke. He never should have said a thing. He had imagined his father would do what he had done when he was drinking. Now everything was worse and he felt ashamed. Nobody can fight your battles, Dale thought. That's what it came to. Maybe when you're ten years old and you're being picked on by some skinny man with a tub of a wife. Not now though. He was on his own now and if battles were going to be fought, he'd have to fight them himself.

Burke and Bothner, Dale thought, in new anger. They held just about every card. All he had done now was put his father on the spot and make him feel bad. For nothing. What was his father going to do with his plant supervisor? With a man who had everything—who was the size of a stupid horse besides?

Dale wanted to make up, and returned to the kitchen.

Alcohol. The certain smell was there, and his heart sank. The smile on his father's face was too friendly, too. "How're things coming along in there?" his father said.

"Fine," Dale said. "I just need another box." Taking one in hand, he returned to his bedroom. He tried to see nothing, to know nothing. But in a moment he caught himself staring at the floor. He had paused in the pushing of jockey shorts and T-shirts into one of the boxes and, returning to himself, felt deflated all over again. What did I ever do to them? a voice within him cried. What did I ever do to any of them?

The new place, partly furnished, had been a garage previously, and, renovated, was what was known as a garage house. The only residence along an alley—in an otherwise crowded neighborhood—it was a flat structure at the rear of a lot upon which the owner's two-and-a-half-story house faced the street. Their address, like others they had had before, was the owner's street number with "½" added. Half of this, half of that; it said who they were, Dale thought.

The owner's lettuce-green Buick Roadmaster, four portholes along each glossy fender, filled the driveway, which led to the street. As Dale was carrying some boxes around to the kitchen door on that side, he was shouted at by the owner, Mr. Barton. Dale had placed a bucket with broom and mop handles sticking out not far from the kitchen door and the green Buick, and the man had appeared at once at his rear porch door and called to him, "Don't let that stuff hit against my car." Dale only nodded.

The appeal of the place, his father explained, was privacy. No one lived above or below, or on the other side of any of their walls. Privacy. And a place to park, by gosh. In most of their other apartments his father had had to look for a place along the street. Here—as they did with each carload of boxes or clothes on hangers—they could drive into the alley and park next to the side door to the small house. The walk from car to the side door was three steps. Around to the kitchen door was about a dozen steps. Privacy and parking.

Garage house or not, it was hardly different from other four-room apartments they had known. Two bedrooms, a bathroom with a shower stall, and a living room–dining room with a kitchenette on the end where the second door opened next to the landlord's driveway. Stove, refrigerator, kitchen table and chairs, and a bed came with the place. They carried in their coffee table, lamps, his father's bed, phonograph and country music records, Dale's desk and chair, dishes, boxes, clothes on hangers, odds and ends.

Did he like it? his father asked him several times. Did it fit the bill? At least they finally had some privacy. And a place to park.

Dale said it was fine, and it was—moving into a new place, in a new neighborhood, was always a small adventure—at the same time that the little garage house had him going blue and depressed. Its wallpaper had turned brown and was separating from the walls. The square of linoleum covering the kitchen floor was both loose and color-worn in its heavily used locations.

Whenever they had moved—after the first time, which had started out exciting—Dale had fallen into this certain depression, and this was one of the worst. He tried to close himself to it and as automatically as possible went about carrying and unpacking boxes, in his bedroom and in the kitchen, setting up their possessions in a way which approximated the apartment they had just left. He added sheets and blankets to the bed which would now be his, and tossed his pillow on top, trying all along not to let the disintegrating wallpaper get to him. The best part, he knew, would be to look around the new neighborhood. Usually there was a drugstore with a fountain to discover, a neighborhood movie theater or grocery store.

When his father made another remark about taking two buses to school, Dale said he thought he'd give up his morning job sweeping the gym. He didn't get paid anyway, he added. He only did it so he could have practice time in the gym. Saying this, Dale was trying to get above it all, but he seemed not to fool his father.

"Redsie, listen, I had to get out of there," his father said. "This was the best I could do on such short notice. It'll come around for you. I know it will."

"Oh, I know," Dale said.

"They let you take some shots as payment for sweeping the floor?" his father said.

"Yah," Dale said. "Does that sound dumb?"

"I don't know. Having a big gym to practice in is worth something. You know, I don't think I ever realized how much this basketball has meant to you."

"Yeah, well, maybe it's still time to give up sweeping the gym, I don't know."

"Because you didn't get on that team?" his father said.

"Oh, I don't know," Dale said.

His father was looking at him. "You don't want one setback to throw you off track," he said.

"Oh, I know," Dale said. And he said, "Maybe, here, you know, we'll have some good luck or something." He was close to breaking down, though, as the thought of turning things around was on his mind, and his father reached an arm around him and held him.

"Son, you mean so much to me," his father said. "I just wish that was something I learned long before I did. I mean, we're doing okay. But God, I've failed you in lots of ways, I know."

There was the familiar tobacco and alcohol odor-warmth about his father and being held extra tight, as he was, Dale felt again like an eight) or ten-year-old. At the same time, he wanted to tell his father that his dream had been the reverse of that, that his dream had been to help him, to give him comfort and pride, to lift them both up somehow. That was his dream, and now it had been taken away from him.

"I don't know what I can do about Mr. Bothner," his father was saying. "I could go talk to the school principal—that's the only thing I've been able to think of that makes much sense. But you say it isn't a school team, so it sounds like they got you boxed in."

"Ah, it's okay," Dale said. "It's my problem. I shouldn't have brought it up. It's just school stuff, you know. It's okay."

"I feel bad about it," his father said. "You're young, you know, you don't have a whole lot of money, people can walk right over you. Unless they want something from you. If they want you to work for them or go out and fight the battles that need to be fought, put your ass on the line, they'll be nice as can be. Know what I mean? It's one of those things can make you mad as hell."

Within his father's arm, Dale nodded. He knew, he thought. Yes, he knew. He knew, too, that it was all so shameful to him—to be made into a loser when he had worked so hard to be the opposite—that he did not want to talk about it anymore.

"The sonofabitches," his father said. "I tell ya, it makes me mad as hell."

Monday, taking a bus downtown, waiting on a street corner, and transferring to another bus, Dale stared out over the city from the high bus windows as he rode from one side of the city to the other. He looked over his life, too, from the perspective of a new neighborhood and new streets to travel each day. Everything was up to him now, he thought. He should have known that in the first place, still it was something he knew now for sure. He was on his own with Mr. Bothner and Coach Burke. He was on his own in all ways, he thought. Especially now. Here he was. The idea made him feel both cut off and afraid, but it made him feel a little better, too.

From his seat on high, he watched over the street. He did not care to think about basketball anymore, still he thought again of how he had been cheated. Mr. Bothner had stood in the gym and looked things over and decided to take what he wanted and give it to his sons. No matter that they were The Blue Arrows and belonged to someone else. He explained his plan to Coach Burke and stupid Burkebutt said yes, it was okay, what he wanted belonged to and included Dale Wheeler, but he was just a fifteen-year-old boy and Mr. Von Bothner was a plant supervisor and a big shot at Chevrolet and his sons had won the Soap Box Derby so go ahead, take whatever you want.

They took it. They took what was his, and all it was was the only big-deal thing he had ever lived for.

If you have the position or something, Dale thought from his seat on high, nearing his school, you can do that to a kid and nothing will ever happen. If some boy he knew stole things, or broke windows, he might get sent to the Juvenile Detention Home. Even if what was taken or broken could be replaced easily. Even, he thought, if no one was harmed in their heart. But Mr. Bothner and Coach Burke could take what they wanted from him, they could just take his dream and throw him aside, and no one would think for a second of doing anything about it.

For an instant, remembering how he sat on the ball that first day, remembering how cocky he had been, Dale imagined again that it was his fault. He had been so conceited.

71

So blind. He looked down between his feet to the rubber floor of the bus and thought of how blind he had been. Then he saw something else and his heart contracted. He was being punished for thinking he could turn things around. Him and his father. That's what it was. Just because he was an athlete he had thought he could turn everything around, and they just weren't going to let him do it.

Still, it was his dream, he thought, and he had worked for it and what was wrong with a person having a dream? What right did they have to take away a person's dream just because he was poor or because his father drank a lot?

If only it had been his gym bag they had taken, he thought. His sneakers. He might have been mad, he thought, and maybe it would have cost him money he did not have. But that would have been all. He'd have gotten some money somewhere, from his father, and they'd have gone to the store and bought another bag or another pair of sneakers. But there was no way he could go to the store now and buy what had been taken from him. No way. Not now. Not ever.

In school, Dale stayed to himself. He had avoided people last week, when things were at their worst, and he did so again today. Around him, always, there seemed a stampede of others. A new week was under way. The other students might as well have been leaves on branches along the hallways fluttering in the breeze. He was not on the team identified with this school, but he had to walk among them. He kept his eyes ahead, and his heart felt bound by ropes within his chest.

He exchanged some words with his friend Rat Nose, who appeared beside his locker often and who had nothing to do with basketball or with the Michigan Truckers. Words about a movie Rat Nose had seen, words of no consequence, words that Dale knew in a moment he was hardly taking in.

In homeroom, there was Zona Kaplan's glossy black hair before him. In a moment, before second bell rang, she turned her head around and asked if he had heard about the mouse that got married to the elephant. He said no, and she said something else and smiled, and so did he, although he did not understand what it was she had said. Miss Turbush was at her desk in front, just then glancing up, smiling faintly in his direction and returning to writing something down.

An idea came to him. Miss Turbush was speaking, and Dale had been trying to listen to her, at the same time that an idea had started to open its petals in his mind. He could try to join another good team. Not another Whittier district team—which would be easy, and horrible—but a team in another district. It was something he could try. He knew lots of players from other schools, and they knew him, from the park and Summer League and Y League. He'd have to try it soon, though, or he'd end up not playing at all.

There was Miss Turbush, standing as second bell rang, coming around her desk to speak, and as Dale looked at his adored teacher, hope came up in him of going elsewhere in the city, of getting on a team. He really would be a loser if he didn't play at all, he thought. Being a loner was one thing. Being poor was one thing too. But being a loser was something else. He wasn't a loser. That was one thing he wouldn't be. Not him. And he had this idea now. A new idea at last.

One morning later in the week, Dale found the courage, or the opportunity, to tell Slim, the locker room man, that he had to give up the sweeping job. Dale's fear had been that his voice might squeak and he'd start to cry or something. To his surprise, though, parting from the elderly man, he spoke as if in someone else's voice and sounded to himself like any other smartass teenager.

"Know some boy might be interested in the job?" Slim asked him.

"Call Mr. Bothner," Dale said. "His kids could use the practice."

You jerk, Dale said to himself as he walked away. He gave you that job—and you really wanted it—and he's always been nice to you, and you talk to him like that. Like one of the Michigan Truckers, Dale thought. Like Hal Doyle. Like a real jerk.

Moving into the hallway, Dale was blaming his cockiness on his enemies. They had him in a bind and now he was pulling himself down, he thought. He always used to travel on the high road. Where leaders traveled. You could ask anybody he'd ever been on a team with. You really could. He had never acted like that before, because—even if he had never told anyone—he did not believe it was the way a real athlete acted.

Friday, going home after school, turning into the alley, Dale was surprised, shocked some, to see his father's car parked outside the small green garage house. He stopped. The car should not have been there. His father could be bombed, or something could be wrong.

He moved along again. Thinking he had been seen, he could not simply turn away, although turning away, taking off, continued as a possibility as he approached the side door.

Music. Close to the door, Dale could hear one of his

father's drinking standbys, "Good Night, Irene," and he felt both relief and alarm. Drinking. Danger. His father was missing work, and he was drinking. Still, "Good Night, Irene" was one of his on-the-way-to-getting-high songs ("Gonna take another stroll downtown . . .") and could be of the best of times. Later it would be Hank Williams ("Summday you'll call my name/And I whon't answer") and Jimmie Rodgers ("Why did you give me your love, dear,/ When it lasted only a day?") and the atmosphere would be sodden and solemn, red-eyed, unshaven, emotional, unpredictable, dangerous.

He'd get in and out quickly, Dale thought. He was already concerned that he would not be able to use the telephone in the kitchen to try to hook up with another team, and as, opening the door, he heard a woman's voice, he told himself he really would get in and out in a hurry.

"Pop?" Dale said, to announce his presence, adding an immediate lie, as if he had not heard the woman's voice, "Pop, it's me, I have to hurry, have to meet some guys downtown."

There was his father, smiling. He wore a suit, white shirt, tie, and matching vest, and, flush from drink, was fixing another drink. No woman was in sight, however, and Dale wondered if the voice had come from a record.

"Hey, son, you have to do what?" his father was saying.

"Have to meet some guys downtown—didn't you go to work?" Dale said.

However red-faced, his father seemed sober. "Oh, I got sent home early," he said. "Picked up a bruise on my hip where a new die press fell off a cart and banged me a little. Shop nurse said to take the rest of the night off. So me and my old pal, Madeline, standing there behind you, decided to step out for a while tonight. This is my little man, sweetie. Dale, this is Miss, Missus, what in the world do I call you, anyway?"

Dale had looked around. The woman had apparently come from the bathroom. "Call me Madeline, that's my name," she said directly to him. "Boy who is growed up like this, Curly, doesn't have to worry about Miss or Missus, do you, hon?"

She smiled pleasantly and Dale liked her at once. Dressed up, made up, ready for the night ahead, she was pretty in a soft way, with orange-tinted color on her dusty cheeks. Dale did not call her Madeline, though. "Hi," he said.

"Fact, Curly," the woman said, past Dale to his father. "I could call a girlfriend if you like, we could double-date." The woman winked, at him, Dale thought, as he was glancing back around at his father.

Everyone was smiling. His father was moving to hand a glass to Madeline, and Dale was liking her all the more, for what she had said.

"Heck, that's not a bad idea," his father said. "We'd have a time, wouldn't we."

"You a good dancer, honey?" the woman said, looking at Dale sweetly again.

"No," Dale said and laughed. "No, I don't know how." He was pleased anyway with the woman's flirtatious attention.

"Curly, how come you haven't taught this good-looking young guy how to dance?" Madeline said, and she seemed to wink yet again to Dale as she was tipping her glass to drink. "Your dad's a wonderful dancer," she added to Dale.

"I'll tell ya, we went out to Richfield Gardens, we could take him along," his father said. "Young girls there'd be walking on top of each other to get at him."

"How old're you, honey?"

"Well, fifteen," Dale said.

"Heck, that'll do," she said. "We'd have to fib just a little, but that wouldn't be no problem."

"Ah, no," Dale said as—he wasn't sure—the proposition

seemed to be taking a serious turn. "I have to meet these guys downtown. Right away. I'd like to, but . . ."

Madeline was smiling at him still; so was his father. Oh, they seemed to say, we were only fooling. We'd take you along if it came to that, but we knew you wouldn't want to go and we were only having fun.

"I guess a young guy wants to go out with his friends, doesn't he," Madeline said. "Not with the old fuddies who drink too much, play old songs, and generally make fools of themselves."

Smiles, goodbyes, two dollars from his father, and some nice-to-meet-you and nice-to-meet-you-toos followed, and Dale, not having removed his jacket, was on the street again, walking in the direction of downtown. For a block or so, in an afterglow of the encounter with the warmhearted woman, he walked as if he really did have a meeting to look forward to downtown. Reality was close by, however. There was no one to meet, nor any place for him to go. The story of his life. A real leader, he thought.

Again, as he walked, Dale was disappointed over not being able to use the telephone to make his calls. And he was relieved, too. Making the calls, trying to get on some team that had already been put together, he had come to realize, was sure not anything he *wanted* to do. Tomorrow, he thought. He had to do it then, he told himself, or it would be too late to do it at all.

He thought again of a tough boy he knew from summers at the park. Lucky Bartell—his nickname had derived in some way from Lucky Strikes—was a good, perhaps a great athlete and basketball player, and also a right-handed fastball pitcher in baseball. He went to Walt Whitman Junior High, in a part of the city known as Little Missouri, and was one of a gang of boys, tagged hillbillies, who smoked and hung out, wore sharp clothes at times, got into fights, had scrapes with the police. They were boys nonetheless with whom Dale had always been at home—their families, like his own, had moved north from Missouri and Arkansas, from the Ozarks, to work in the auto factories—and they had played on sides hundreds of times in three-on-three and half-court games at the park, and they knew him, too, to be a good athlete. What would he say, though, to someone like Lucky Bartell? Why would any of them, especially the good players from around the city, want to add anyone to a team which had already been formed?

An hour later, Dale was sitting in the balcony of the Strand Theater, watching the first half of a double feature. In another hour, he was still sitting there, although he wasn't quite sure what he had seen. A cowboy movie. There would be cartoons and previews and MovieTone News of the World with Lowell Thomas, and the second movie would be a cowboy movie too.

Dale sat there. Gunfire and hoofbeats. Dan Duryea. Walking home around ten, Dale could recall Dan Duryea's certain voice, and he could see the flat-brimmed cowboy hat he wore, and the string around his chin, but he could recall little of anything else from the two movies. All he seemed to know was the feeling of loss it gave him to sit through two movies, or even one, when there were so many other things he wanted to do.

Saturday, when the time came to make his calls, Dale was more nervous than he would have expected. Why would another team, if it was any good, want some outsider to join them? What would he say? New rejection. Humiliation. That was all he could see coming back to him over the telephone. Everything would be made worse. He'd gone a week without weeping to himself against a tree like a baby, and if he made these calls, all that would happen is he'd be put back in a hole again and feel like some dumb lost dog wandering around.

Nor was it Saturday morning, but late Saturday afternoon when he finally sat down at the telephone. His father's bedroom door had been closed earlier—it was usually left ajar—and although Dale had not heard the woman during the night, he hadn't heard any music either, which wasn't like his father, and on the chance that she was there, Dale left to give them time to get up and do as they wished. At the park he played three-on-three much of the day, between trips to a walk-up drive-in two blocks away for a Coke and a milkshake. It was a brisk October day and radio snippets of a football game—Michigan State was playing Michigan—touched the air from passing car and house radios, and the players who came to the park were older and slow and not serious about the game. Around four he left to make the long walk home.

Finding the boy's name in the telephone book, Dale experienced cold feet again. He couldn't do this, he thought. He just couldn't. How could he come off as anything other than an ass kisser? The lowest of the low—a brown-noser, a suckass. It was the worst of things to be in his world, and was something, he was convinced, he had never been before. He'd never been chicken and he'd never been an ass kisser. His record was clean.

There were two Bartells in the book, and Dale was trying to imagine everything going smoothly. He wanted to play City League. What would he do if he did not? He might as well give up everything he had ever worked for and tell the Bothners they had just pushed him out of the way.

Lucky Bartell was known as a hood. Not a park rat, like Dale, he still played often at the park under the lights during the summer. But he drove a car to the park—apparently his father's—although, like Dale, he was in ninth grade and, as far as Dale knew, had yet to turn sixteen. But he was a hillbilly, too, as most everyone from Little Missouri was, and the hillbillies did about as they wished when it came to driving cars and other acts requiring maturity. A girl who married and had babies at thirteen became an adult in the grocery stores of Little Missouri, and so did her seventeen-year-old husband, going for a job in one of the factories, become one of the men along the streets and around the repair garages.

Lucky Bartell also smoked between games during the summer, which was not unusual, and sometimes he came to the park wearing not a white T-shirt but a red or maroon Banlon polo shirt, its collar turned up and its buttons unbuttoned at the throat. The expensive shirts reminded Dale of a time the previous year—they were only in eighth grade—when the Walt Whitman team came to his school to play and Lucky and two or three other Walt Whitman players showed up wearing dark blue double-breasted overcoats over rayon dress shirts without neckties, and they looked just like the tall seventeen) and eighteen-year-olds who played for the big city high schools. And in a fist fight which broke out one night at the park, Dale had stood with a mob of other boys and watched Lucky Bartell duck and bob and smack his fists repeatedly into the face of a much taller high school boy—a high school star, in fact—who had come along with friends to play and had apparently believed he could lean on and push around the younger, smaller junior high school boy who had such a growing reputation.

Dale had known, had sensed, as the problem developed, that the tall boy, Butch, was going too far and that Lucky Bartell might surprise him. It was Lucky's cool. There was always something in his faint and faintly mischievous smile, and in his politeness, and when he said to the tall boy, "Tell you what, Butch, I'd advise you to get offa my ass or I am going to have to teach you a lesson."

Butch guffawed, said, "Hear the hillbilly talk—you talk funny, man," and the game continued, and Butch kept going too far, kept pushing and testing. A moment came when Lucky stopped, placed the ball on the surface of the court, and said, "I gave you fair warning, man, so you'd better do what you can to defend yourself."

Butch needed a moment before he said, "Whatever you say, hillbilly." And as they moved toward the grass beside the court the cry went out, "Fight! Fight!" and play at the other end stopped too, as everyone came running to watch.

Dale just knew, although he did not know why or how he knew. Lucky Bartell had his reputation for fearlessness, in addition to his certain cockiness and certain sense of humor, and they had played many times on three-man teams together, but Dale had never seen him fight. Still, he knew. There was something certain in him, just as there was something speculative in the older boy, no matter their differences in age and size.

Fists up, they circled. "Butch'll kill that kid," someone said. "Kick his ass," one of Butch's friends said.

"Get him, Lucky," Dale heard himself say, and saw one of the high school boys fire a glance his way.

Butch may have been older, at an age when two or three years meant so much, and he may have been a high school star and some six-three, one-seventy to the junior high boy's five-ten or -eleven, one-forty or -fifty. But none of his advantages or his lanky reach translated into strength or really knowing how to fight, and he was at once in over his head as Lucky Bartell, chin tucked, snapped one fist and another, and found the tall boy's eyes, chin, nose, mouth, forehead so certainly and sharply that the fight was over in a minute or two, although it lasted five or six or seven. They were not knockout punches, however cleanly they smacked into the taller boy's head and face, but the sharp blows damaged him so quickly that blood was running from his nose, and his lips were broken and bleeding, and it was clear that he was in a sad hole from which he did not know how to extricate himself. Only as both of his eyes were all but closed and his face, neck, and the front of his shirt were covered with blood did he hold up his hands and say, "Enough, okay, hillbilly, you win, enough."

Lucky Bartell put on a small show as the crowd dispersed and the tall high school boy and his friends slunk away. Removing a long comb from the carpenter's ruler pocket of his blue jeans—as he often did—Lucky ran it through his glossy black hair, returning it to its glistening duck's tail. In his soft accent, reminiscent of Andy Griffith, grinning his grin, he said, "Well, let's play some ball, ain't that what we're here for?"

"Dale Wheeler?!" Lucky said when he was called to the phone by his father—whose voice sounded like Johnny Cash—at their home over in Little Missouri. "Cain't be you, man, Dadah's bullshitting me for sure."

"It's me," Dale said. "How you doing, Lucky?"

"Shoot, doing okay—what're you doing, man? What's happening?"

"Oh—I got this problem," Dale said, wishing at once that he could just hang up.

"What problem is that?" Lucky said.

"Oh, I really got screwed here in City League. I got squeezed off the team I thought was actually my team, you see. What happened is this guy who's a plant superintendent or something at Chevrolet, he came along, he just showed up at our school, he has two sons, and he had a sponsor all ready and everything, some company he owns or something, and what he did is he signed up Joe Dillard and everybody but me, because, our school coach even told me this, because I was better than his one son, because he didn't want anybody to beat out his son for a position. So I just got cheated is all, I didn't even get to be on my own team, so right now I'm not on any team at all."

Dale paused, and at last Lucky said, "Shoot, that sounds like a drag."

"Yeah," Dale said.

"Sounds like they hung your ass out to dry, you know?"

"They sure did," Dale said, noting a similarity in his father's words and voice and those coming over the line.

"So—?" Lucky said. "You're looking for a team to hook up with?"

"That's what I was wondering—if you guys might have a place. You know?"

At last, upon a pause, Lucky said, "Heck, we got our ten already. We're pretty much all set."

"Yeah, well, I guess I knew you would be," Dale said. "I just thought I'd give it a try. I mean, you know, don't think I didn't know that. I didn't want to ask, but I sorta had to. They just—well, anyway, I know what you're saying."

"I wish I could help," Lucky said. "Their team ain't gonna be as good without you on it, I know that."

"Yeah," Dale said. "I was—dreaming of winning the City."

"Well, you'd have to get by us," Lucky said.

"Oh, I know," Dale said. "Well," he added, wishing he could simply disappear. "I understand. Thanks anyway, Lucky."

"I didn't do anything to be thanked for," the boy said.

"Well, you know what I mean," Dale said, at a loss for how to escape. "Listen, good luck in City League. I'll see you."

"Hey, good luck, man," Lucky said. "I'll see you."

The receiver replaced, Dale sat and stared over the tabletop and tried to contain himself. He was on his way to filling up again, he knew, and he stood up then to go and do something, to get away if he could from the feeling coming up in him.

That's that, he was saying to himself. He wouldn't do that again. Not ever. He'd go downtown, he told himself. That's what he'd do. He was okay. He'd get out and go downtown and go to another movie.

Trying to convince himself that nothing had happened, that he had not made a fool of himself, he moved into the adjacent living room and slipped on his windbreaker. Stopping by the bathroom as if by habit, to take a look at himself in the mirror on the way to going out, he was unable to look up at his own face. Standing over the sink, he tried to raise his head to look, but there occurred a corresponding tightening in his heart and neck and he knew he couldn't do it, short of breaking down. Just when he had thought he was okay, he thought, Jesus, he had to do that, and now he was messed up again. In addition to all else, he was angry that he was still this way, that he had so little control over himself. Pull yourself together! he thought. A faint gasp escaped anyway as he tried, as an act of will, to look up at the face before him in the mirror.

He turned to leave. Screw everything! he said to himself, heading back across the living room toward the side door. Screw everybody, too! Getting away seemed the only way to escape the feeling, and he was at the side door, doorknob in hand, when the telephone rang.

He paused. The phone rang again.

The phone rang a third time as, turning back, Dale returned to the kitchen. "H'lo," he said.

"Wheeler, Lucky."

"Lucky," Dale said.

"Man, listen," Lucky said. "I just talked with my daddy, and he said—ah, hell man, you're on our team. If you wanna be. That's why I'm calling. Ole Dadah said it sounded like you got a royal screwing—and he said to me why didn't we just go ahead and put you on our team, as an added player, 'cause people do get sick and all that

sometimes. Anyway, Dadah's right. He usually ain't anywhere near right, I have to tell ya, but I could see this time
right away that he was, you know. I just had to think about
it or something, or have somebody else say something.
Anyway, you're on our team if you wanna be."

"Really?" Dale said. "Really—oh, God. Thanks a lot.
You're sure it's okay?" Still again, his eyes were filming
over, although this time with happiness.

"It's okay. Shit, man, I'm the captain. We just coach
ourselves, you know, no sponsor, nothing fancy. Anyway,
Dadah was right. I only needed a minute to think about
it."

"It won't cause any problems?" Dale said.

"Nah, it's fine. I know you're a real good player. Don't
worry. We'll be glad to have you. It's no problem."

"Ah, man, thanks," Dale said. "Really, thanks a lot. I
don't know what I would have done."

"This guy's some big-shot rich guy?" Lucky said. "That's
what you said?"

"Yeah, he's plant superintendent where my father works.
And he owns some company or something which is going
to sponsor the team. And I guess he used to be some big-
deal basketball player or something himself."

"People like that, they think their shit don't stink," Lucky
said. "I'll tell you. Just once—every once in a while, you
know—I'd like to meet some rich person who wasn't such
a asshole. Know what I mean? My daddy says they do exist,
although he's never met one his-own-self. You know—rich
people are the worst athletes, and they're the biggest chick-
enshits, always. Why is that? I'd sure like to know."

"Yeah, me too," Dale said.

"This guy just came along and took the whole team to
give it to his little boys like a present?"

"That's what he did," Dale said.

"That dirty sonofabitch," Lucky said.

"Yeah," Dale said as, in another sudden rush, he covered the telephone to conceal the sound of emotion coming up in his throat.

"Anyway, Little M's is cool," Lucky said. "That's what we call ourselves. Little Missourians. I'll just tell everybody what happened and what a good player you are, although most of them know that already. Heck, man, in school league, we always figured we just had to stop you and Joe Dillard and we had it made. Even our coach said that. So it'll be okay. Just come over to Walt Whitman gym on Saturday, we have our game at nine-thirty, and I'll have your name on the roster."

"Ah, thanks," Dale said. "Thanks a lot. You're saving my life."

"You're a good player, man. You'll just make our team better. Don't mention it no more."

"The Little M's?"

"You like that? Little Missourians. It was my idea."

"My dad's from Arkansas," Dale said, feeling pride in something he had never felt pride in before.

"Is that right?" Lucky said.

"Only we never lived in Little Missouri. We lived just about everywhere else around here, but never there, unless it was when I was real small."

"I knew there was something redneck about you. Shoulda known. That's cool, man. Welcome to the Little M's. We stick together. We're rough and tough, hard to bluff, cain't get enough a that wonderful stuff."

Dale laughed, smiled, feeling the emotion stirring again in his throat.

"That's our motto," Lucky said. "One thing you cain't ever get enough of is that wonderful stuff."

"Yeah, I know what you mean," Dale said.

"Okay, man, gotta go. Fact, my old man's standing in the doorway looking at me right now, which means he probably heard me say a swear word or something. Dadah, why the hell you looking at me like that? Can I help it I was born so goddam good-looking? Anyway, I'm gonna have to get off the phone I guess and kick Dadah's sorry ass is what I'm gonna have to do. See you Saturday, man—about nine. Bring sneaks and stuff, orange jersey if you got one, 'cause that's gonna be our colors. Orange and black, take no flak. Always show up, always fight back—the Little M's."

"Orange and black," Dale said. "Okay. Orange and black."

"See you Saturday."

Off the phone, Dale stood there, trying to take in what had happened. Orange and black? He was on a team again, and the awareness of it thrilled him. A good team. New friends. A new chance. Just as he had never felt lower than he had earlier, it seemed now that he had never felt higher. Each time the problem seemed to be to keep himself from going to pieces.

At school, Dale did not mention to anyone that he was on a new City League team. He still felt ashamed of himself for being left off the team from his own district—would always feel ashamed—and being on a team from another part of the city only called attention to the fact. And he felt embarrassed. Why would Zona, or Rat Nose, or Miss Turbush not think there had in fact been some reason why he was left off the Michigan Truckers? He wasn't about to mention the Little M's around here. No way.

At the same time, the Michigan Truckers were mentioned everywhere, up and down the hallways, on the sidewalk before the school, in the locker room, like it was the new hit song of the year. Dale could understand why; he still thought the Truckers' name was the coolest name he had ever heard. But then, when he heard it, it hurt and he tried to close a door to himself.

Overhearing remarks in the locker room, Dale learned that the entire team had gone to the Bothner horse farm the previous Sunday, to learn how to ride horses, to eat "mounds" of fried chicken—Gump Gardner, he heard, "ate nineteen pieces of chicken!"—to see home movies of those certain Soap Box derbies, "the Nationals at Akron," as the phrase was repeated like the chorus of the new hit song. "The Nationals at Akron. The Nationals at Akron. The Michigan Truckers and the Nationals at Akron."

Michigan Jerks, Dale thought.

He said nothing, though, tried not even to think anything in response to what he overheard. He tied his shoes, stepped under the nozzle to rinse his hair, pushed his tray along in the cafeteria, passed the ball, followed the pass, moved without the ball. Jealousy and resentment still gathered within his face and neck, however, and several times he passed the ball with such ferocity that it ricocheted from another player's hands, and more than one of them said, "Jesus, take it easy."

Dale's emotions seemed erratic. The two brothers might have been his friends, too, he'd think at times, and he would have liked them and been pleased and proud, too, to tell of their winning the Soap Box Derby, and of their horses and fried chicken. Then he would feel so much resentment for the two, would think of them as cheaters, and of the father as the dirtiest liar and cheater of all, that he would fantasize beating up all three of them at once in a fist fight, during which fantasy, in the heroic moments of his flashing fists, his eyes would gloss over and he'd have to bite his lower lip to retain composure.

His feelings about Sonny Joe and his other one-time teammates were different now, too. They had left him and betrayed him. Still, they seemed to have no idea that it was so unfair or of what it had done to him. They just went along with the rich Bothner brothers and their stupid tubs of fried chicken and it didn't mean anything to them that one of their regular teammates had been cheated out of being on the team. How could they do that? Dale asked himself often. How could they just go along and pass him in the hall and talk in front of him as if nothing had happened?

He asked himself in time if it was simply jealousy which made him feel as he did. If someone else had been left off the team, would he have gone to the Bothner farm and stuffed all that fried chicken into his mouth? Would he laugh and be thrilled that he had new friends who had almost won the Nationals at Akron?

The thought bothered him. He could see himself doing what the rest of them were doing. Feeling privileged, too, it seemed. Believing it was all okay. Yeah, too bad about so-and-so, but that's the way it is. Those things happen. He was sorry, but what could *he* do about it?

No, Dale thought at last. No, he wouldn't have done it. If it wasn't fair like that and if he had any idea that someone was being destroyed by being left off a team, he wouldn't have done it. He'd been captain lots of times, on lots of teams, and he had always made sure that everyone got to play.

He'd have spoken up about it too. He always had spoken up about things like that. Because that was what a captain did. He was a real athlete, and a team leader, too. He thought of things, and that was sure something he'd think of. Whenever some overweight or awkward kid got left sitting on the bench, he was always the one who saw to it that they got to play. Look at all the times he had done that. You could ask anybody, because it was true.

Sonny Joe Dillard never did anything like that, because he might be a captain but he wasn't ever a good captain. Look at the time Bobby Lymon's parents came to see Bobby play, in Y League, and Dale took himself out and put Bobby

in, even though Bobby Lymon was the fattest kid in school
and spent most of every game sitting on the bench. Look
how Bobby Lymon came up and thanked him, and how
he'd been surprised because he wasn't looking to be thanked
at all. It was how he thought of being a captain. Because
he'd rather be loyal than anything at all. It was true that
he hadn't thought of it all that much before now, still it
was what he'd always done. Because he'd rather be dead,
he thought, than be slime like that, like Coach Burke. That
dirty liar. The coward he was for not standing up to Mr.
Bothner when he came to steal a team. How could he not
say, no, I'm sorry, Dale Wheeler has been one of my best
and most loyal players and his dream is to win the City,
and this is his year, and I'd never do that to a young boy.

It's what Miss Turbush would do, Dale was certain. She
had more balls than Coach Burke, that was for sure. She
might be a little white-haired lady, but she sure had more
balls than stupid Burkebutt. She had real balls, in fact, and
Burkebutt didn't have any at all! That dirty fat chicken
coward. He'd rather be dead than be a fat little chicken like
that, Dale thought. He really would. He'd rather be dead.

More days passed, and still no one said anything to him
about what had happened. On Friday, to his surprise—it
was a small shock—Zona Kaplan raised the subject in
homeroom. There early, as he tended to be, having given
up the gym-sweeping job, so was the dark-eyed Zona there,
among a few others.

"I thought you were on the basketball team but I heard
you aren't anymore," she said.

As always, Zona was carefully made up. (So beautiful
was her smooth skin, her touches of rose blush, her flesh,
her earthworm-colored lips, that she reminded Dale of a

little girl's exotic doll and of fancy pastry, too, in the window of Schrimer's Bakery, there so close to him that she looked good enough to reach to with his tongue and lick.) At the same time a certain shock was in his heart over what she had said.

"The school team I'm on," he managed to say. "It's the City League team I'm not on."

"What's the difference?"

"School team's sort of rinky-dink," Dale said. "They only play eight games and they never have play-offs. City League goes all the way into March, and has play-offs and a big play-off at City Auditorium for the whole city."

"Oh," Zona said.

It was as if she still did not understand, and not wanting the subject to just slip away, Dale said, "On the school team, in fact, I'm co-captain. Me and Joe Dillard are co-captains. But on the City League team I'm not at all, because, well, I'm not." Not on *this* team had been his thought, but he was not ready yet to say that he had transferred something like his loyalties elsewhere, to low-life Walt Whitman and the hillbillies of Little Missouri. Zona would never understand, he was sure.

"I always heard you were a really good player," she said.

Well, she understood some things, Dale thought, as he thought to reconsider. Turning more in her seat, though, she was moving, leaning closer to speak, and in her nearness, her aroma, his mind seemed to go blank. There were her faintly red cheeks, her unpainted lips, the faintest shadow above her upper earthworm, the whites of her eyes as white as the enamel of a stove, centered by their deep brown buttons. "Don't tell anybody," she whispered. "We're going to have a party. We're inviting everybody on the team, too."

"Who's having a party?" Dale said.

"Sshhh!" she said. "I said don't tell!"

"Oh," Dale said. "Oh, I won't."

His experience was limited to a few elementary school birthday and Halloween get-togethers, and parties were not something he knew much about. He was aware, though, that they had started to happen this year, and the excitement they aroused in him was as real, perhaps, as it was in most anyone. "Where's it going to be?" he whispered, leaning toward Zona as she was returning sideways in her seat.

"We're not sure yet—but don't tell anybody!" she said.

Dale looked up to see Miss Turbush enter the room. She glanced around; at her desk, she removed papers from the briefcase-style bag she carried. Miss Turbush, as Dale knew, always came into homeroom in the morning with some expression or question, or joke even, ready on the tip of her tongue. It was one of the reasons Dale liked her as he did, besides knowing that she liked him—a couple teachers in elementary school had also liked him; others since had more or less ignored him—and he watched Miss Turbush now, a faint smile on her face, in anticipation, Dale knew, of whatever it was she was about to say.

Things are sure better now, he thought, as Miss Turbush stepped to the closet to hang up her coat. Zona Kaplan's glistening black hair was close again, too, as his focus shifted. Not in smooth ropes today, it was combed so its ends curved under and out of sight. Not a single hair seemed out of place and the mass of silkiness gave off an oil-on-water sheen of green and red. A thought came to Dale, a desire, to touch her hair as he had touched it those times when it was in braids. To squeeze it. He also thought to smell it. And he decided to do it, for the desks around him remained mostly empty and he was hot to do it.

He extended his face toward the glistening mass. There was the aroma, a freshness, a strain of perfume, too. He experienced the old secret charge within. And he imagined Zona Kaplan's intimate secrets close before him, her dark nipples, a puff of hair below her belly, and he imagined her belly button, too, a cavity upon a plain of Jell-O. "Your hair is really neat," he whispered all at once—another charge was set off in him—close enough to her neck that the words might slip, it seemed, under her cascade of brilliance and up, easily, into her ear.

He had only embarrassed her, he could see, as her shoulder moved away.

"Dale, you seem awfully close to your neighbor this morning," Miss Turbush said suddenly from the front of the room.

Dale flushed—his face felt like a cooked tomato—as he also laughed. Miss Turbush was smiling, watching him, amused. She knows, Dale thought. She seemed always to know, but she never disliked him for what she knew the way other teachers did.

"We're looking a little devilish this morning, Dale," she said.

"We are?" Dale said all at once. "Me?" he added, awkwardly, but pleased to enter into any kind of banter with his adored teacher.

"You, indeed," the white-haired lady said. "Is there another Dale here?"

Dale kept smiling, and he said, all at once, "Miss Turbush, you're the one—I think—who's devilish. You're always like that."

She laughed with pleasure, at his daring, he imagined, and he laughed, too, with enjoyment he had hardly ever known. He felt so much better today.

"You think I'm being devilish?" Miss Turbush said. "You may be right, Dale. You may be quite right about that. I had a very nice walk to school and I am in a devilish mood this morning. But I did not mean to embarrass you; I assure you I was only teasing."

"I wish all my teachers were like you, Miss Turbush,"

Dale heard himself say—however red-faced—as even more of the barriers he had always known with teachers were falling away.

She appeared to take added interest in this; she even stepped around her desk, as if for a closer look. "How is that, Dale?" she said. "I hope you don't mean I'm easy."

"You're nice," Dale said. "Mean, but nice, too," he added in a flustered attempt to make her laugh, as she had before.

"*Mean?*" she said, in mock surprise. "You think I'm *mean?*"

"No, no, I'm just teasing," Dale said, as if she had been serious. "I mean—you're the one that, you know, that makes us *want* to do the work all the time."

"Oh, well, I knew what you meant," she said. "I was only teasing you—a little, because you flattered me, and *embarrassed* me, in what you said."

"Heck, I wish you were my mother," Dale said, heard himself add without thinking to add it. He felt, knew at once, that he had gone too far—he could see that Miss Turbush felt the same way—as Zona shot a glance back over her shoulder.

Miss Turbush turned to two girls just entering the room, the two Sandys, Rowe and Chase, and she looked to her desk, too, where she picked up a paper. "How would your mother feel about that?" she added, looking at the paper before looking up at him.

"Don't have one," Dale said.

"Well," Miss Turbush said. "Maybe we've exhausted this subject for right now." She said good-morning to someone else entering the room, and continued working at her desk as if nothing had happened.

Dale looked to the windows, red-faced again and aware that he had overstepped a line. It's because I'm sort of crazy right now, he thought. At the same time, his heart ran on with affection or love for the white-haired woman. It felt good, no matter what, he knew, to have said what he said to her. However he had embarrassed them both, he thought she had liked it too. Only then did Zona Kaplan glance around at him—as still other students were entering—and say, with the faintest of smiles, "I can't believe some of the things you say!"

The three top players of the Little M's, its front line, smoked in the locker room. It seemed the coolest thing to do, to smoke as they dressed, and during the halves and after showers, too. They were Lucky Bartell, with his Andy Griffith twang. And Chub Coburn, the biggest player, the team's burly center, whose face was acne scarred and who had a similar twang. And the other forward, lanky Grady Devlin, who smiled with flawless white teeth on the way to anything he said, which he always said slowly and mischievously. Lucky smoked Pall Malls; the other two smoked Camels, Chub usually bumming from Grady, who never objected. However soft their voices, the words which came forth were as undiluted, as defiant and tough as the boys themselves were rumored to be.

The dominant team in the Walt Whitman district, they won games with ease, one after another. After games, after cigarettes, showers, more cigarettes, they left to go their separate ways, to go home, to go downtown, or to wander along Corunna Street and hang out at the pool hall there, or at a railroad car diner, or at the corner gas station where Chub Coburn had a job pumping gas Saturday afternoons. The gas station owner and an attendant, two men in blue uniforms, spoke with the same easy Ozark twang and rather than mind, seemed to enjoy having the gang of teenagers hang around for an hour or two, to listen to their stories, their outrageous bravado, to smile and smirk, to work in an occasional remark, and occasionally to rock with laughter at some audacious claim of strength or courage, speed or daring.

"That sonofabitch looked right at me like he figured he was putting the fear of death in me or something," Lucky might say of some teacher or policeman, store manager, bus driver, or girlfriend's father. "So I just smiled at him and I said, well, is that a fact, and made like I was gonna turn away, ya know. Then I just come around and nailed that sonofabitch. Knocked him cold. It's true. Ask Grady. God's truth—ain't it, Grady? Knocked that guy out cold, flat on his ass."

Hanging out was different from what Dale had known at his own school, and he liked it at once, liked the outrageous stories and accounts, liked simply to laugh with such new pleasure. He listened and almost never talked. Sitting in the bleachers with his teammates or in a booth at the diner, or leaning among the old peanut and pop machines, the cigarette and candy bar machines and cluttered metal desk in the gas station, he listened and felt warmth in the company of these others, these new friends for whom he felt such new affection and admiration.

Storytelling was always at the center of things. So was *listening*, unlike at his own school, where, after games, most everyone stood around and pushed and bragged, bickered and blamed, or, usually, went off to be picked up by a parent. More than he wanted anyone to know, Dale enjoyed listening to the stories. He *loved* listening to them, in fact, for what they seemed to do to him, although he could not have told anyone what it was. The stories made him feel good, he knew that. Some were heroic, or touching, or incredible, most were funny, and Dale managed to believe them all, if he knew them to be true or not.

He did not smoke. In the beginning, a number of times, he was offered cigarettes, but felt no temptation to accept.

After all, he was an athlete, and he remained too serious about basketball, probably too self-conscious, too, to give in to that allure that most boys and not a few girls at the time did not face until their first year at one of the city's big high schools. Lucky, Chub, Grady, and a couple others, cupped paper matches in their hands to light their cigarettes, tapped and flicked ashes here and there, held burning cigarettes in the corners of their mouths while they squinted and spoke cockeyed, gave every impression, Dale thought, of being adults who happened to be in junior high.

Dale laughed often too. At times, he feared he might be laughing too much, and he tried to moderate his responses. It wasn't that his laughter was false, and he was aware of a need in him to laugh, being more extreme than it might have been in others. Then, again, one of them would tell a story or say something and he would try to contain himself, even as he often felt so happy or amused he would gurgle foolishly and his eyes would fill with tears.

In an exchange then after the last game before the Christmas break, Dale heard something in his voice he had not heard before. They were in the locker room, his teammates were hurrying along for reasons having to do with Christmas, and Dale was actually talking, telling of a cafeteria incident which had taken place at his school. In his own voice, though, what he heard was the familiar twang of Lucky, Chub, Grady, and this surprised him. It sounded false, even as he heard himself doing it. It made him feel false. Even that he was talking at all had to do, he knew, with the fact that it was snowing outside and everyone was hurrying off to do Christmas things and he did not want to go off alone. Christmas with his father, as always, would be booze and blues, Jingle Bells and heartache.

Being a *phony* was one of the worst things to be. It was right there next to being a *suckass*, and was something Dale had promised himself never to be. Being a phony was nearly as bad as being *chicken*, or *queer*, conditions so bad pre-

97

vailing belief had it that one so burdened might as well kill himself and get it over with, because there was nothing ever to look forward to but misery and shame.

If it wasn't bad enough to hear what he had just heard with his own ears, Dale found himself suddenly challenged by Chub Coburn.

"Wheeler, don't talk like you one of us, 'cause you ain't," Chub said, a small, mean smile on his face. "You laugh too much, too, man, all the time. That's ass-kissing, and I don't go for somebody kissing my ass."

"Screw you!" Dale finally said, however lamely. "What's that supposed to mean?"

"Shoot, I don't know," Chub said, looking away. "I don't have any idea at all what hit is supposed to mean. Do you, Grady?"

Grady may have glanced, but, kindly, did not reply. Dale felt stricken. These were his new friends. They meant so much to him; that was why he laughed so hard. They made him laugh. He liked them. "Screw you, Chub," he added. He would have said more, he thought, if he had only known what to say. He didn't. Chub said nothing more, simply ignored him, perhaps aware of how true to the mark his words had been, and in a minute, trying to conceal how hurt he was, Dale said, "Gotta hit the road, see you guys after New Year's," and as some of them said so-long, he moved along the aisle with his gym bag to leave.

Outside, waiting for a bus as new snow was falling, hurt was so certain within him that he thought of going back inside and announcing that he had decided to quit the team. Anything to save face. He did not turn back. He could have cried, he felt so awful, but he did not cry, either. He boarded the bus and rode downtown, where he walked around, to see if he could get something else, anything else, to go on in his mind.

It's Mr. Bothner, he thought. And Burkebutt. If they hadn't done to him what they had done, well, he wouldn't be in a dumb situation like this. If he was on the team he was supposed to be on, he wouldn't be messed up and talking like somebody else, and laughing too much, and he sure would not have anybody on his team making him look like a fool. If they did—if somebody spoke to him like that— they'd go outside and fight, and he'd go in with every confidence of knocking the person's stupid block off, no matter how big they might be. Even Gump Gardner, the big second-string center, wouldn't talk to him like that.

What a prick Chub is, Dale thought, although his thought had little fight in it. Why'd he have to say that? It was so mean. Were they mad after all because Lucky had let him be on their team? Was that what it was? Or was it because they had seen how much it meant to him? Was that why he had been such a phony? Jesus, he hated himself.

Other things had been said to him by other Little M's players, and he began to brood on those, too. Emmett Booker, a good guard and the one with whom he was increasingly paired, said to him once in the locker room, "Dale, how come you live with all those rich people when your own people—leastways it's what Lucky told us—is from Arkansas?"

Emmett Booker was one of only a couple Little M's who did not smoke or hang out after the games.

"I don't live with rich people," Dale had said. Was that what they thought? That he was one of the regular Whittier Junior High kids? "In fact," he said to Emmett, "we used to live right up the hill from Chevy Plant Four. Although we don't live there anymore. Not everybody who goes to Whittier is rich, that's for sure."

"They ain't?" Emmett said.

"Emmett, goddammit, I told you Dale got *screwed* by that rich guy!" Lucky said from along the aisle, as if to explain something yet again to a child.

"We got rich people here, too," Lucky said another time in the locker room. "RICHER, in fact, I'd say—wouldn't you, Grady?—wouldn't you say there are people here who are richer than those rich people over at Whittier? Just about everybody who lives on the other side of Miller Road is rich as hell. A course we just kick their asses anytime they act up, even though they ain't *all* bad. Chub—Conrad Zimmerman's not so bad, is he, for a kid who's really rich?"

"Lucky's in love with his sister," Chub, standing at the end of the aisle, said to Dale, to them all. "That's why he says that, 'cause he wants to talk about her. Gives him a thrill, ' 'cause I still get a thrill . . . talkin 'bout you!' " Chub sang out. "Yeah, Conrad Zimmerman's okay," he added. "Can he ever swim. Conrad Zimmerman can swim in fact like a goddam fish, hit's true."

"It is true, what Chub says," Lucky said, slipping into the heart of their common Ozark drawl. "I am in love, I am, in actual point of fact, deeply in love with Doreen Zimmerman. So let's talk about her, 'cause Chub's right, too, when he says talking about Doreen Zimmerman gives me a thrill. It is giving me a thrill, right now. Tell me this, though, any a you uglies. You was as good-looking as me, you was half as cool and tough as me, and Doreen Zimmerman was in love with your ass, wouldn't you be in love with hers at least a little? Wouldn't it be stupid not to be?"

He paused, looking around, waiting for a response. "Wahl?" he said. They grinned, enjoyed the question, but none—in the face of such apparent truth—dared reply.

"She is only about the best-looking thang in the en-tire United States of America," Lucky said. "It's true. It just is. What's more, y'all should know, 'cause it's important. What's more—she is *more* in love with me than I am in love with her! Which is the way it should be, and is the way it always will be with me as regards women. The woman—and there will be lots of them after my ass; one look at me and that should come as no surprise—the woman, the women, will always be the ones who is more

in love with me. That is not to say I won't be in love with
some of them, sometime, because maybe I will. Being in
love is fun. It feels good. I tell you that 'cause I know none
a you has been around enough to know what love is all
about. Tell you, never forget for a minute how to treat a
woman. You gotta be a little mean. And very cool. Which
is why so many women is always hot after my ass. 'Cause
I know how to treat 'em. I know how to make 'em really
feel good. Always makes me laugh, I tell you, I see some
guy treating some girl like she is queen of the ball or something. I go up, I want to, take away a girl like that in about
one minute. I look like Clark Gable—wouldn't you say?
Well, I know I do, so it don't matter if you agree or not.
That's how I treat women. 'Frankly, my dear, I don't give
a damn.' Women love that. I can have just about any
woman wild about me in no time if I want to. It's true,
goddammit, so don't laugh. A course, I may have to kick
some boyfriend's ass, to show it really is true, but that's
sorta fun at times and ain't never been no problem. Grady,
tell Little Wheel about the tennis tournament I won last
summer. Go on, tell him. He's a redneck, but he probably
won't even believe it."

Lucky, smiling, looked to Grady, who smiled his easy
smile. Others also seemed to pause, adjust ears, and slow
down to listen. It was story time.

"Well," Grady said slowly, showing his white teeth.
"What it is, ya see, is there is this fancy tennis club, up on
the other side of Miller Road." Grady was speaking more
or less to Dale, as Lucky had told him to. "It's the Racquet
Club or something, this real snazzy place for members only
where rich people swim in their big pool and play tennis,
you know, and sit around in the sun. Well, Doreen Zimmerman—and she may be the prettiest thang in the whole
world, Lucky ain't too far off when he says that. To see
Doreen Zimmerman is to melt. Ya know? She is that pretty.

And she ain't no easy chick either, in case you might be getting the wrong idea and think she is. She is class. Real nice girl. Innocent little old thang, what she does, bless her heart, she takes this no-account redneck, self-centered, conceited Lucky Bartell as a guest, you know, to her snazzy ritzy tennis club because her parents are just too polite, too dumb, I don't know, to let her know that this is not anything anybody in their right mind oughta do."

This line in the story—perhaps new—drew laughter from Lucky as he sat listening attentively, and laughter, too, from the others.

"What happens a course," Grady says, "is Lucky gets hisself drawn into entering this fancy club's tennis tournament even though he is just a guest for one day. Okay, it's just the fourteen and under tournament he gets entered into, it ain't like it's the Michigan State Open or something. At the same time, though, this is last summer and it's true, Lucky is close to turning fifteen. Thang is, these boys at the fancy club, they know about Lucky, they know he's a star, you know, and they think, well, what they will do is whip his ass good in this one sport about which he knows next to nothing and put the redneck in his place once and for all.

"What happens then—which is funny, 'cause Lucky has never even held a tennis racket in his hand, let alone play the game. What is funny is this one boy decides to complain and say this guest cain't be in their dumb tournament 'cause it's members only. And I don't know just exactly what happens next, 'cause I wasn't there a course, but as I understand it, someone of the big shots there says, well, that's okay, son, we can use us another player to round things out and why should we worry about a guest anyway, especially one who ain't even ever played the game before?! A course the guest is Lucky Bartell, which don't mean nothing to that dumb sonofabitch, and he even says what he has to say right there in front of Lucky, that it don't matter, that he'll just get knocked out in the first round anyway, and that way, he says, one of them will have a easy match and nobody will have to draw a bye. Idn't that what he said, Lucky, with you standing right there?"

"That's what he said," Lucky said. "He didn't even smile either like he thought it was funny or anything."

"A course, he doesn't know who it is he is dealing with, like I say," Grady said. "He sure don't know what it means to say something like that right there in front of all them boys in their little white suits. A couple of them do know, a course, 'cause they know who Lucky is. Well, I guess I have to say it, even though the redneck no-account is standing right here in front of us. Lucky Bartell just may be one of thee best, if not thee very best athletes I've ever known, personally, to take up a ball or glove, or anything else, at least in the Walt Whitman school district.

"Heck, you can guess the rest, otherwise I wouldn't be telling you this. Who wins that first match and has to return the next day as a guest to play again? Who wins that day, too, and has to return still again the next day? As a guest. Who wins another day, too, and another, and is finally crowned fourteen and under champion of the fancy tennis and swim club and is given a trophy that is about yea tall? You guessed it. Redneck Lucky is the one, and what does he do when it is time to be given the big trophy? He says just one minute, please, and he takes his comb out of his pocket and combs his hair back like he's a movie star or something, and then he says okay, I'll take that trophy now." The concluding hair combing detail had them all tittering, as Grady added, "Only you tell Little Wheel how you did it, Lucky."

"Tell ya this," Lucky said. "Where they made their mistake was letting it go on for days like that, that and that guy talking like he did. All that time, what it did was give me a chance to think about it, you know, 'cause, like Grady says, I can do about any sport there is better than most people to begin with and, shoot, you give me a week to learn it, then you better be goddam good or I'm gonna kick some ass. Which in fact is just what I did."

"At's true," Chub said. "Lucky may not be worth a shit for much of anything else, but one thing he can do is play sports."

"Whatta you mean not worth a shit for anything else?" Lucky said, flicking cigarette ashes. "Who the hell's Doreen Zimmerman in love with? It sure ain't some UGLY mother like you, I'll tell you that."

It was then that Lucky squished out his cigarette on the floor, where it joined one of half a dozen or so, and stepping to the end of the aisle, all at once called out, calmly, "OCKIE!"

The others, Dale noticed, pulling off jerseys and untying shoes, began to giggle and snicker, and glance to the end of the aisle. Ockie, the locker room man, a thin-haired sixty-year-old janitor who walked with a shuffle-limp, appeared in a moment with broom and dustpan.

"Ockie would you take a look at that floor," Lucky said to him.

Ockie looked down, as instructed, and continued to stare at the mess of butts and ashes.

"Idn't that a mess?" Lucky said. "That is shameful, and what I'd like you to do, Ockie, is get busy with that broom of yours and sweep that mess up. Ockie, this here, by the way, is Dale Wheeler, who we call Little Wheel, come over from Whittier Junior High to play for the Little M's."

Ockie raised mainly his right eye to glance at Dale, the newcomer. The man had a near-smile on his face, and Dale gave a nod, as if to say hello. The other boys, Dale also noticed, even as they looked aside or tried to conceal the sound, were still tittering.

"Ockie," Lucky added. "Y'all wouldn't want Little Wheel here to go back over there to his school and tell everybody there is cigarette butts on the locker room floor at Walt Whitman Junior High. You wouldn't want that, would you?"

Ockie stood there; he appeared perplexed, amused, not ready to give in. Then, it seemed, he blinked an eye.

"You better get it cleaned up then, hadn't you?" Lucky said.

More of a grin came to Ockie's face as he readied broom and dustpan in separate hands to do the job. But first he leaned slightly toward the rest of them, and they all seemed to pause. "Little summbitch ain't half as smart as he thinks he is," Ockie said in a raspy near-whisper, and—this was it, what they had waited for—gurgles of laughter broke forth, from Lucky as much as from any of them, and as Ockie went on to sweep the butts into the dustpan, and strolled away, the boys were so stricken they staggered and leaned to the lockers, weeping with laughter—actual tears ran down Lucky's face—and Dale could not help laughing and weeping with them.

That afternoon, downtown, in freshly falling snow, Dale continued occasionally to giggle. As he waited to step down from one bus to cross the street and transfer to another, a man beside him in factory clothes, holding a black metal lunch bucket like his father's, remarked, "Shore is coming down today, ain't it."

"Shore is," Dale said.

Off the bus, carrying his gym bag away into the falling snow, holding back as long as he could, Dale laughed, then giggled as he tried to check his laughter. "Little summbitch ain't half as smart as he thinks he is," he said to himself. It wasn't very funny, really, which was why it had been so funny. Dale had never been a smartass, nor did he know if he could be one now. It had been a long time, though, since he had felt as good as he was feeling. If only it would last, he thought, suspecting, of course, that it would not.

Waiting within a V-shaped store front for the connecting bus, out of the heavy snowflakes, Dale kept tittering. As he stepped back to the sidewalk, to look for his bus, a young soldier, a paratrooper in a brown uniform and glossy, bloused boots, turned into the store front, removing his cap, flicking away drops of snow and water. "Kid, hey, tell me something, will ya?" the soldier said.

Dale looked and listened.

"Where's the action around here?" the soldier said. He was twenty or so and was fixing his cap back onto his all-but-shaved head. "Gotta be some action somewhere in this town."

"Gee—the action?" Dale said. He wasn't quite sure what was meant.

"Yeah, women, you know. Wine, women, and song."

Dale smiled. There was the soldier's brown uniform, a single row of ribbons on his chest, a paratrooper's insignia, other insignias and patches. "The only place I know of," Dale said. "There's this bar, around the corner, in the alley down here. I've seen women go in there a lot. But mostly later, at night. I don't know about this time of day."

"You going that way—point it out to me, will you?" the soldier said.

Dale said sure, although he had not been going that way. They walked out and along the sidewalk together, and he felt self-conscious and proud, too, walking with the paratrooper.

"Saturday P.M.'s not a bad time," the soldier said. "I'll tell you that as a tip for when you're older."

"Saturday P.M.?" Dale said.

The soldier nodded, breathed into his bare hands to warm them up as they walked. "Mainly it's 'cause that's when women are out," he said. "They feel like it's safe to fool around a little, you know, 'cause it's daylight still and their old man thinks they're at Sears buying nylon stockings. Shoot, it's all a game. You'll find out."

"At Sears buying nylon stockings?" Dale said and smiled.

"Or ice cube trays," the soldier said. "Something like that. You'll find out."

Dale pointed up the alley to where the bar was located. "See that sign," he said. "I think it's kind of a fancy place, but I'm not sure. Back on the main street there, you go down about four blocks, there are all kinds of bars. Only they're sorta honky-tonk hillbilly places. There are a bunch more, about three quarters of a mile to the left, it's Chevy Corners, but they're sorta honky-tonk too."

"Well, I'll try the fancy place first, I guess," the soldier said. "Although I'll probably end up down in the sleazy joints."

"What're you doing in this town?" Dale said.

"Oh, just passing through," the soldier said. "Chasing rainbows. You'll find out. Listen, thanks for the tip—hey, let me give you a buck for your trouble." He was removing his wallet.

"No, that's okay," Dale said. "Forget it."

"No, no, I want to."

"No way," Dale said. "Not me. Good luck."

"Hey, I could use a little luck," the soldier said, and he winked as he started up the alley.

Dale turned, too, and started back. It came to him as he walked along that his voice had slipped back into the Little Missouri twang there at the end and he saw himself for a moment as an empty shell, a blank space. Of the soldier, he thought, Jesus, that looked great. To go along like that, by yourself, Dale thought. Looking for action. He wondered if it was the uniform. The uniform made it seem like the soldier wasn't alone. Like he was with someone, Dale thought.

The woman, Madeline, was there for a time that afternoon, and that night, calling Dale from bed for fresh cinnamon doughnuts, his father said to him, "Son, I been meaning to tell you something. I read in the paper somewhere that all kinds of cheating goes on in those Soap Box derbies. It's the way a lot of those cars get built, because it's the fathers who do the building and not the little kids who drive them. What it is, I guess, is the fathers lie, and the kids lie, too, 'cause they know they didn't build the cars, even though they know they're supposed to, while the ones who do it fair and square, well, they generally don't ever win."

Dale felt uncomfortable as his father related this, as if it was something he had gotten away from, to some degree, and did not wish to return to or hear of again. Still, he said, "You think the Bothners cheated?"

"Well, I don't know that," his father said. "I'd only say that the father's an engineer. He's a man who wants those things for his sons. And he's a man, too, who has made it clear he won't let things like fairness get in the way of what he wants. Do I think he cheated? I guess I think he did, although it's not anything I could ever prove."

Dale had stopped eating his doughnut. "I don't even like to think about it anymore," he said. "It makes me sick to my stomach."

"Well, maybe I shouldn't have told you that," his father said. "I don't think there's anything to be done about it. I just thought it might make you feel a little better, but I can see how it wouldn't, too."

Dale nodded, faintly, to agree. The old misery was in him again, as it hadn't been for a while now.

"Some things are just better forgotten, I guess," his father said. "Don't let it make you bitter, though. You know—don't do that."

Dale nodded, to say that he knew when in fact he did not. What he did know was that the sickness was calling up the misery, and there was that familiar feeling of being left off the team coming up in him again. The unfairness.

"I talked to this paratrooper downtown," he said all at once. "He asked me if I knew where the action was."

"That right?" his father said, amused.

Dale did not know where he was going with his report. "He told me—you could pick up women on Saturday afternoon because their husbands thought they were at Sears buying nylon stockings."

His father laughed. "What did you think of my little friend?" he said.

"That lady?"

"Madeline," his father said. "I guess you could call her a lady."

"I thought she was nice," Dale said. "Yah, I liked her. Do you like her?"

"She is nice," his father said.

"You mean you're gonna get married?" Dale said, to tease his father.

"Oh, no, my gosh, I don't think so," his father said. "That's not what I'm gonna do. No, I just wondered if it bothered you, my bringing her home like that—ya know?"

"Doesn't bother me," Dale said.

"You sure?"

"Well, maybe it makes me a little nervous," Dale said. "But it sure doesn't bother me."

"Makes me a little nervous too," his father said, and laughed. "I mean she's my old pal, and she's a sweet woman.

But you come first in my life. I want you to know that. If something like that bothered you, I just wouldn't do it."

"Well, don't worry about it," Dale said.

"Well, I won't, if you say so," his father said. "By the way, anybody ever tell you you're a good man? They haven't, they ought to."

One day after school that week, Dale was stopped by the landlord, Mr. Barton. Some days Dale approached the house through the alley and others, especially if he circled by one of the stores in the neighborhood shopping district, he used the landlord's driveway, usually passing beside the man's green Roadmaster as he walked to the garage house in the rear. "Hold on there!" he heard someone call from inside the house, and he heard, too, he was certain, "Those goddam lazy hillbillies." Shocked, knowing but not knowing that he had been addressed, Dale continued walking.

Hearing the side door open behind him, Dale glanced back. Mr. Barton, the landlord, was holding the screen door. "C'mere a minute," the man said to him and looked down to wait for him to return.

Reluctant, Dale walked back the half dozen steps.

"Why don't you bring in those garbage cans when you come in here? You can do that. You live here."

Dale looked at the man. His father looked after their single garbage can, which he put out about once a month. "Those aren't ours," Dale said.

"Doesn't mean you can't bring them in, you come along here like that," the man said.

The man frightened Dale. He resembled Coach Burke in size and age, but Dale did not know what he did for a living. He owned the big Roadmaster, even if it was usually parked there, day and night.

"Hear what I'm saying?" the man said. He was nodding, smiling then, as if Dale were simpleminded. "A boy like you. You'd do well, you live in a decent place, to take a little pride and do stuff that needs to be done."

Dale was irritated, but also confused and intimidated. "You want me to carry in your garbage cans," he managed to say. "I don't mind. I'd do that. I don't like somebody just telling me what to do, though." However defiant his last words, Dale remained uncertain of himself, and he knew, too, that he was conveying uncertainty in his voice and in the way he averted his eyes.

"Anybody, you southerners, I'll tell you something, you'd do well, you live in a decent place, to do the things that need to be done. People won't say you're lazy."

Dale looked back at the man. Lazy?

"Understand what I'm saying?" the man said, smiling again, using a mocking voice as if speaking to a child.

"Not really," Dale said.

"I'm telling you, you come by here, I'd like you to carry in the garbage cans they're out by the road—capisch?"

Dale kept looking at the man, who kept looking back. Dale, then, was the one to blink. His only salvation in the incident, he thought afterwards, was that he did not say anything more. There he was, walking back to the street, hating himself already as he did so, where, schoolbooks in one hand, he picked up the two lids and placed them on the smelly cans. It's what it was to be a boy, he was thinking. Jerk like that will just tell you to do things. Just because they're older they think they can tell you to do anything and it's like you have to do it. The jerk.

Books under one arm, he carried the two cans back along the driveway. Mr. Barton had returned inside his house and closed the door. Was that laughter he heard? Dale wondered. He wasn't sure. Hillbillies. He had sure heard that. And he knew he was trying in part of his mind to make believe he had not. It was as if he would not have to feel insulted, and therefore would not have to fight back, as if he could make himself believe he had not heard it.

Placing the cans next to the small rear porch at the rear of the main house, Dale went on his way to the garage house. There was their single garbage can, in place as always, and passing it now, he felt like kicking it, in sudden anger not with Mr. Barton but with himself. That jerk made a fool of you just because you're a kid, he thought.

City League game days, Saturdays, became the best days of the week for Dale. As his position on the team grew more certain, so did he look forward all the more to the arrival of the weekend. And so did he get up and leave earlier, to make his way, riding two city buses to Little Missouri, where he was happy to be.

His pattern was to stop at the P & O Diner on Corunna Street, to have toast or a muffin and a pint of chocolate milk, maybe to run into one of his Little M's teammates with whom, in time, as daylight was breaking, to walk over to the school locker room to get dressed for their game. The first times he stopped at the diner, in November and December, the morning sky was still dark. Now, even earlier, the sky was light and sometimes there was narrow morning sunlight.

Sitting on a stool at the counter, Dale placed his gym bag between his feet, swiveled some on the stool, and enjoyed the warmth of the diner. Country music played from a small brown radio just beyond twin coffee makers where one glass tube bubbled brown and the other bubbled clear. The counterman, a thin man in his forties with sunken eyes, was usually friendly and usually said, "How ya doin' there?" or "Mornin' there," as Dale settled upon a stool and loosened his jacket, as he settled into the coffee and cigarettes atmosphere that Little Missouri seemed always to offer. Never having been treated warmly in a public place, Dale had a thought more than once that it was a way to live forever.

One morning, the counterman said to him, "Son, ya know, you had my money, I had your looks, we'd both be a whole lot better off'n we are." Something in the man's voice reminded Dale of his father's voice.

Then, a fiercely cold morning in February, when Dale had made his squeaky walk from bus to diner and ordered hot chocolate, the counterman, placing it before him, said, "Hear tell your name's Wheeler and your daddy's from down in Arkansas."

"That's right," Dale said.

"Where'bouts in Arkansas?"

"A town called Paragould," Dale said.

"Bill Wheeler?" the man said.

"Yeah," Dale asked. "Are you from there?"

"I shore am," the man said.

"Really?" Dale said. "You know him—you know my dad?"

"More or less, I do," the man said. "I'd say reasonably so. He's got a couple years on me, and we weren't ever fast friends, but I think he'd know my name."

"What is it?" Dale asked.

"Louis Treadway Junior. Tell your dad, tell him you ran into Louis Treadway Junior, see if it rings a bell for him. Hit is a small world, hain't it. Tell ya this, your dad was quite a man about town in Paragould, certainly before hard times come along and his daddy lost their store."

"Their store?" Dale said.

"Wheeler Dry Goods," the man said. "Hain't never told you that?"

"Wheeler Dry Goods?" Dale said.

"Right in the center of town," the man said. "Name's still there in fact, chiseled in stone, 'cause I happen to remark on it last time I was down there, which was only a year ago Fourth of July. A course that whole block is owned now by that Currier clan and I believe the actual dry goods store in fact has become some kinda real estate and insurance business."

"Maybe it's somebody else," Dale said. "I never heard anything about that."

"Well, gosh, I hope I ain't telling something out of school here," the man said. "I'm pretty sure we're talking about the same people, though. Warn't no other Bill Wheeler from Paragould that I ever heard of."

"He never told me about Wheeler Dry Goods," Dale said. "I don't know. Maybe it's somebody else."

"Well, as I say, I hope I haven't betrayed a confidence," the man said. "You got me worried about that now. Could be, though, he just forgot!" the man added. "People do tend to get caught up in what is happening now, as opposed to what might a been happening in the long ago."

Dale shrugged, to more or less agree. His father, he knew, talked at times about his early years in Michigan, landing the first job he had had in years, or ever, late in the Depression, at Chevrolet Motor Company. He almost never mentioned anything about his life before that.

"A course, like I say, we wasn't ever fast friends or nothing. Still, tell him you ran into Louis Treadway Junior. I think he'll know me. Tell him, he's in the neighborhood, you know, to stop by and say hello, have a cup of coffee."

Dale nodded that he would, but as the man moved along the counter, something told him that stopping by the diner—in work clothes or even in one of his three-piece suits—was something his father wasn't likely to do. Dale also realized how secretive his father was. How proud, too. Maybe their voices were alike, but his father just wasn't at all like this man, Louis Treadway Junior. In fact, Dale realized, his father wasn't like any other men or fathers he had ever known. What he was like, in his secretive ways,

Dale thought, was someone in exile, like a Russian count or something, in hiding, working in a factory, letting his life just slip away.

Then Dale thought, questioned, in pleasant surprise, *a store!? Wheeler Dry Goods!? Chiseled in stone!?* Thought and image were like found money, and Dale was experiencing a gleeful feeling unlike any he had ever known. To own land and buildings. A business. Did it mean you were somebody, he wondered, rather than nobody? His father was a nobody, he knew that. Factory workers were nobodies. But a store! A dry goods store!

He did not know what it was like on that side of things, Dale thought, but he sure knew what it was like on this side. The Little M's, they were on this side, and the Michigan Truckers were on that side. The workers and the bosses. Soldiers and officers, as his father had said. Soldiers who died, Dale thought, so the officers could live, so they could go home and act like heroes. It was a pretty good deal for the officers, for the Bothners, Dale thought, just as he knew without the slightest doubt that theirs was a side on which he could never stand. He knew, just like that. If they had ever owned a store or not. The knowledge was in his heart as he sat there in the P & O Diner, early on a frozen Saturday morning. And when he looked again, it was still there in the reflection of the coffee urn. It all had to do, he saw, with why he had wanted to win the City in the first place. To turn things around. For him and his father. To show them all that they counted too.

That afternoon, when he returned to the garage house, his father was gone. Dale was disappointed, because he had wanted to talk to him—he had more on his mind than just the dry goods store in Arkansas—although he wasn't sure what it was he would say. Would he try to explain his thoughts of that morning, of all the mornings now before games when he had gone to sit at the diner as day was breaking? It had been exciting to have the thoughts he had had, to experience ideas, and he wanted to do it some more. Miss Turbush, he thought. His father might hear him, or not. Miss Turbush, he knew with certainty, would hear and would, in some interesting way, open his eyes to something else.

What happened at home—it was a certain hazard being there alone as the sky grew dim on a Saturday afternoon— was a rising up into his system of Zona Kaplan. He fantasized necking with her. He yearned, perhaps fiercely, to neck with her. For necking was what was done, entered into by both boys and girls, almost as a game, and, as it was possible, it was how he longed to be with her.

What you did, he told himself, was you got alone with a girl, and you worked up the courage to say something, or to touch her, maybe her hand first, or her elbow, perhaps her shoulder, and if she did not resist, you put your arm around her, and if she still did not resist, you turned her head, and this meant it was time to kiss. Necking could commence. Necking and teasing. As an end in itself. If she moved her lips into that first kiss. He had done it a few times—the best had been lying on blankets in a tent at the lake one afternoon last summer with a thirteen-year-old girl he had met half an hour earlier—although each time he had tried to go on to the next step, which was to feel the girl's breasts, he met with resistance. Still they were hot times, French-kissing and rubbing and pressing, even if, as it was said, nothing really happened. Something not quite happening, as Dale was learning in other ways, too, might be a form of something happening after all. What he wouldn't give, he thought, to have nothing happen this afternoon with Zona Kaplan.

He telephoned her. His father wasn't likely to return—

he was probably already into his weekend bar-hopping drinking pattern—and with the telephone to himself, and the sudden confidence, or desire, Dale sat down to call. He hated to sit around on Saturday afternoon anyway, and he looked up Zona's number and dialed quickly, before he had a chance to think about it.

"It's me," he said, when Zona had been called to the phone. "The good-looking guy who sits behind you in homeroom."

"Dale Wheeler?"

"Right on both counts," he said.

"What?!"

"I was wondering what you meant that time you said you couldn't believe some of the things I said," he said, scrambling to respond to a degree of irritation in her *what?!*

She laughed. "I do remember that," she said.

"So do I," he said, relieved.

"That's what you really want to know? That's why you called?"

"Yes, that's why I called," he said. "I been thinking about that ever since you said it and I had to call up and see what you meant."

"Well—I meant just what I said."

Her tone was not unfriendly, but her remark seemed to close a door on being silly, and he was at a loss for what to say next.

"When are you gonna invite me to that party?" he said, as it seemed to pop into his mind.

"What party?"

"That party you told me about."

"That was a long time ago."

"Oh."

"That was back when we talked about it."

"Oh."

"So how are you? Is that why you called?"

"Aah. No. I just called is all. You already had that party?"

"A long time ago. Weren't you there—I thought you were."

Even as this stung, he managed to say, "Let's see, maybe I was. I'm not sure. I go to so many parties I forget sometimes which ones I go to."

She laughed, although not with the richness he had heard at school. "Where are you—at home?" she said.

"Yeah."

"Where do you live? I don't even know."

"Oh. Well—I don't live where I used to. By Chevrolet Avenue. We moved a while ago."

"Oh."

"Well."

"That's a deep subject," she said.

"Yeah. I just called—to say—I like to look at your hair, in homeroom."

She laughed again, faintly still. "You say all those crazy things," she said.

"It's true," he said. "Sometimes I touch it. Only you never know I'm doing it."

"You do—really?"

"Sometimes, if I feel like it," he said.

"That's why you called?"

"No. Sorta. I—I called because what I'd like to do is touch it again. Right now."

"What's that mean?"

A wire fence had come over her voice and he knew that she was no longer amused. "I don't know," he said. "It doesn't mean anything. I mean, I'm just joking."

"That sounds sort of icky."

"I said I was joking. Don't you have a sense of humor?"

"I always thought I did. Before now."

"It's clean, isn't it?" he added, thinking the only way out was to push ahead.

"Clean? Is what clean?"

"Nothing, forget it," he said.

"Yes, it's clean! Listen, I have to go. I'll see you in school," she added, almost nicely.

They said goodbye, and replacing the receiver, Dale paused there in the stillness for a minute. What was in his mind, in addition to the humiliation he felt over the disappointing phone call, was a sudden suspicion that the two Bothner brothers had gone to the party. Would the girls have invited them, and therefore not invited him? The girls of his ninth grade class? It was nothing he wanted to think about anymore, because in the center of his heart he already knew the answer.

He took up the telephone again. It was another chance, and something was telling him not to do it. Looking to the telephone book, he dialed Lucky's number. In his mind was an image of meeting up downtown with some of the Little M's. Anything to get away from the person who had just talked like an idiot to Zona Kaplan.

"Lucky, it's Dale Wheeler," he said when, as before, the boy's father had called him to the phone.

"Little Wheel, what's going on?"

"Oh, nothing. Listen, I'm just calling to see if you guys are doing anything tonight. You want to hang out, go to a movie downtown or something?"

A pause followed. "Heck, man, cain't do it tonight," Lucky said. "What I'm doing is I'm going to a party over to Doreen Zimmerman's, and truth is I played all kinds of hell getting her to let Grady come over. Know what I mean? Heck, I'd invite you, you know, except it's Doreen's house, and, well, like I said, I played hell getting her to let Grady come, because this girl for Grady, you know, Carolyn Frost, she's gonna be there, and the problem is, two low-life rednecks is about all they'll put up with at one time on that side of Miller Road. You know?"

"Oh, sure, I didn't mean that. I just meant, you know, if you guys weren't doing anything, that was all, if you wanted to go to a movie or hang out or something, that was all. I don't wanna go to any party. That's the last thing I wanna do. I was just thinking of going to the movies is all."

"Won't be long, it'll be play-off time," Lucky said.

"Yeah, not long," Dale said, even as he was aware again of a subject being changed.

"You about ready?" Lucky said.

This didn't even sound like Lucky, and Dale said, "Oh, sure," then, "Listen, I'll let you go. I just thought I'd give it a shot is all."

"Looks like we'll play Lowell in the first round," Lucky said.

"Is that right—Lowell?"

"Yeah, they're winning their division about as easily as we're winning ours, and I guess that first game we'll get to play at home. Anyway, hey listen, take it easy now. I gotta go."

"Yeah, take it easy," Dale said. "See you Saturday."

As Dale replaced the receiver, the feeling he had anticipated was flowing into him, an aftertaste of being brushed off. Oh, it's not so bad, isn't any big deal, he told himself, still the feeling of rejection was there within him like a warm liquid. Everything had been fine before he called, and now it wasn't. It was so dumb to make calls like that. What should he do now, he wondered. Should he grab his coat and walk over to the small business district close by to hang out for a while, or should he go downtown and look for some way to waste away the evening? What was the best way to get away from himself and from everything else? Those dumb Truckers, he thought. They had been his friends. They just went along with the Bothners and left him hanging dry like this.

. . .

An urge—actual thought—to light up and puff a cigarette came to Dale in the locker room after gym class on Monday. Smoking cigarettes was always a question or an accusation. Do you smoke? Who smokes? He smokes, she smokes. Dale had puffed a few times, behind garages, inside garages, along alleyways with other mischievous ten-year-old boys and girls. (Touching into other forbidden areas as well, for when it was time to sample the forbidden, one door seemed to lead to another.) Dale had never taken on an entire cigarette, however, or smoked in public or bought cigarettes, or inhaled without coughing, or thought to violate that code wherein he regarded himself as an athlete.

What got to him was not the party to which he had not been invited, but another party. Sitting on a bench, removing his shoes, he overheard Hal Doyle say, "No, no, what I heard is Bothners are going to have a party this time because Zona Kaplan talked them into it!"

Dale might as well have touched electricity. A shock ran into his hair. He took a breath, sat and stared between his feet. He felt a dozen miles away. The Bothners had come along and taken everything. Zona had gone over to their side too. She had been the object of his dreams, and he had told her how they had cheated him, and she had gone, without a thought, it seemed, and with a smile on her face, over to the other side.

Dale returned to his shoes. The urge came up in him to light a cigarette. He'd like, he thought—like Lucky, Grady, Chub—to walk among the Truckers with a cigarette in his mouth. Up yours, the cigarette would say. Perch on this, you twerps, the cigarette would say.

Dale imagined, too, being at one of their dumb parties and lighting up and smoking in the same cool way that

Lucky smoked in the locker room. He'd be the only one smoking, of course, at a Whittier-Bothner party, and the girls would run off shocked, but maybe thrilled in a way, too. *"Dale Wheeler is smoking a cigarette!"* And he'd be told by some bossy girl, or by some parent, to put it out, or to take his filthy cigarettes with him and leave, and that's what he'd do. And maybe one of the boys would give him some crap, too, in which case he'd say, "Why don't you come outside and tell me about it." And he'd turn and say to all of them, on leaving, "Up all your asses with a ten-foot pole, you bunch of twerps."

What occurred in fact, as he stood to continue undressing, was a catch in his breath. And a thought deep within, saying: I never did anything to them and they're cutting me out of everything.

Well, he wouldn't start smoking, he told himself. That really would mean they had beaten him, and he wasn't going to be that easily knocked off. Screw that. One thing he was was an athlete, he was certain, and it had nothing to do with any of those jerks. He worked at it and it was true. He knew it was. If they were going to beat him, they had better come to play. If they were going to beat him, they'd have to beat him on the floor, where it counted.

Nearing home after school, Dale saw the empty garbage cans ahead along the curb and his heart felt seized. He had nearly forgotten the previous incident. If the cans had been out on other trash days, it must have been when he entered through the alley. What was he going to do now? A fear was in him that if he walked by, and walked down the driveway without picking up the cans, Mr. Barton would storm out and call him a hillbilly again.

At the same time, he did not want to pick up the man's garbage cans. Something in it was submissive in some way, as if he were chicken or something.

Still, what if the man talked to his father and they both thought he was just a smartass teenager?

He walked by. He turned into the driveway and left the cans behind. Nothing happened. His ears and neck seemed to burn as he walked down the driveway past the side door, but nothing happened. By the time he was at the garage house, however, he felt oddly in agreement with the charge that he was a smartass teenager, at the same time he felt better, he knew, than he would have if he had trucked along the guy's smelly cans.

In the morning, as always, Zona was there before him in homeroom. There was her glossy black hair, a faint perfume in the air about her. His heart felt squeezed as he realized he liked her now, again, more than he had liked her before. She had him now. It hadn't been so bad to sit behind her when she had only brushed him off on the telephone. Now she had him. She had sold him out and gone over to the other side. His crush on her had been like an autumn day. Balmy and pleasant. Now it was like a thunderstorm and she had his heart in a vise.

He loved her. That's what it was. He felt certain the pain he felt was love. There was a warmth in him, and it felt good at the same time that it hurt. He could almost lean forward, close to her neck, and say something to her again, anything, even as he knew it would turn her off all the more.

. . .

There were seven or eight of the Little M's—he would never be certain—and they picked him up at the Texaco station two and a half blocks from where he lived. The call came from Lucky on a school night, late in the evening, just as Dale was starting his homework. "Little Wheel—that you?" Lucky said. "We're picking you up in ten minutes. Tell me some easy place, close to where you live."

"What is it—what's going on?" Dale said.

"Can't say right now," Lucky said. "You'll see. Tell me a place."

"Team meeting!" Chub's voice called out in the background, to an explosion of laughter. "Tell him it's a team meeting!"

Dale did not consider not going, even as something in the call told him he would do better to stay home. It was already ten to nine, late to be going out on a school night, and he had all of his homework yet to do. He could use that as an excuse. Still, it was his team, his teammates, and he had no feeling to say no, no matter what it meant about his homework.

At the same time, taking down his red and gray athletic jacket, he paused, knowing that something unusual or illegal was in the air, aware, too, that the jacket might be identifiable. He slipped the jacket on anyway, added his cap and gloves, and went out into the chilled February night. Jacket's no problem, he thought as he hurried along. Its colors belonged to one of the big city high schools and it was nearly a uniform among boys his age.

The car, driven by Lucky, rocked to a stop in the gas station almost at once, and was filled, overfilled with laughing, excited faces. A four-door Mercury, two doors opened on the side closest to Dale, releasing a blast of cracks and laughter and warmth from a crush of bodies on bodies. "Team meeting, Dale, let's go!" "Time to haul ass, Dale!" "Load it up, man, let's roll! Little M's team meeting!"

Four faces were in the front seat and, as Dale was pulled

into the back, on top of others, the door was pulled shut and the car rolled on again, reentered the street, rolled along. Dale knew by now, knew from the special excitement, although he did not know how he knew, or that he knew for certain. Into the roar and crush, and from within his own fear and excitement, he called, "What's going on? Where we going?"

"Team meeting!" several voices yowled. "Little M's team meeting!"

Dale knew, just as he knew he was giving them lines to which to respond. "What kind of team meeting?"

"Grady, tell Little Wheel what kind of team meeting!" Lucky called from behind the wheel.

"Fat Frankie's gonna get us up for the play-offs!" Grady said.

An explosion of laughter filled the car.

"Who—where?" Dale called.

"Man, you're sitting on her!" Grady called and this brought a new burst of laughter, and remarks, too, of "No, no, I'm not her, get your hands off me!" and "That's not a pussy, that's my dong!" and more laughter.

"Frankie!" Lucky called from his driving, and the voices let up some to listen. "Tell Little Wheel about our team meeting! What you gonna do, Frankie?"

The mob of them waited in anticipation.

"Talk like that, ain't doin' nothing'!" a girl's voice said from within the crush of bodies.

"Oh, Frankie, darling, honey, please don't tease my doubtful heart!" Lucky called out, to fresh laughter. "Don't break my heart, now that you got me in such a state and I need you so bad it hurts in my pants."

"Just don't talk dirty, that's all," she said. "You won't get nothin' from me you talk dirty."

"Whew! What a relief," Lucky said. "Had me scared there, Frankie. Got such a hard-on, don't know what I'd do!"

This brought new laughter, more howls and cries of "Oh, God, I smell fish" and "I can't hold it any longer!" and "Drive faster!" and "Let's get where we're going!"

"Get where?" Dale called.

"Don't worry, we'll be there in a minute," Lucky called back. "Frankie, you ready to go steady?"

"Dale, I bet you're still a cherry, ain't you?" Chub called over his shoulder from the front seat.

Dale didn't say. He made believe he had not heard the question. Lucky called out, "Frankie, darlin', you there, darlin'? Tell Little Wheel how many times you gone steady with the Little M's."

As before, the mob quieted some in anticipation of the girl's reply.

"Come on, Frankie, just asked you a simple question. Can't you count, darlin'? How many times. I just want to see if you know how to count."

"Seven!" she said at last, petulant.

Laughter exploded again, and Lucky called back, "Frankie, darlin', you sure it's seven, or is it twenty-seven?"

"You just keep your mouth shut!" the voice said from below.

"Dale, what about it?" Chub called out. "You didn't answer my question. Shoot, man, I know you're a cherry, I can tell, or you woulda answered."

"Who is—you are, Chub?" Dale said, although lamely.

"Just answer my question, don't try to play games," Chub said.

"Well, maybe I am, but if I was, it wouldn't be any of your business," Dale said. "So maybe I'm not. What do you care anyway?"

"Are you or not? It's a simple question. That's all."

"Up yours, Chub, get the hell off my back," Dale said, knowing it was a risk, knowing that the next exchange might be the last before a fight.

"Hey, enough, you guys, enough," Grady said. "Get off his ass, Chub, for chrissakes, we're just having a good time."

"I just wanna know if it's his first nooky, that's all," Chub said.

"Awh, Chub, you're riding his ass, so lay off—let's be teammates," Lucky said.

"Why you so interested in where my pecker's been?" Dale said.

Laughter from this was better and reassuring to Dale, into which Chub said, "Shoot, I know you're cherry, man. I just want to hear you admit it is all."

"*Goddammit, enough!*" Lucky said. "This is a team meeting!"

Chub said nothing more. Neither did Dale. They all know the truth anyway, he thought. No doubt about that. And what returned to the center of his mind, as Lucky had turned onto a darker street, and onto another, which was dirt or gravel, was what was about to happen.

Lucky turned the car again, into an even darker location, the wheels rolling over hard, bumpy ground.

Well, it's going to happen, Dale said to himself, and could not quite believe it. It's going to happen. As if his mind had sealed itself off, no other thoughts seemed quite able to get into the center of things. Sex. He was in its grip in a way. He was about to know it and have it, and with a girl. And it wasn't Zona Kaplan, as he had dreamed. A vague sadness was in him over it not being Zona Kaplan, but even this did not quite get into the center of things. His mind was not even the part of him doing the thinking now, he realized, as the car stopped and the motor was turned off. Like everyone always said, his mind had moved south.

. . .

The back seat served as a darkened room. The others stood around the clearing, adjacent to an unlighted dirt road, waiting. Dale stood with them. They joked, talked, made remarks, blew warmth into their hands, acted as if nothing out of the ordinary were happening, that they could as easily be standing before the P & O Diner talking after one of their games. The car door would be heard to open and close in the cool, moonlighted darkness and a figure would approach and someone would say, "Who's next?"

One after another, they walked over and slipped into the back seat of the car. Several minutes would pass. Three. Five. Seven.

Only with Grady, when he had been inside the car perhaps fifteen minutes and time continued to slip away, did attention turn to the car itself. "Hey, what the hell you doing in there, Grady?" someone called. The others laughed. Lucky said, "That's Grady—bastard always takes forever."

Time passed and Grady still did not appear. On Chub's signal, several, then all of them, slipped over and surrounded the car. All at once they began to shout and laugh, to bang and hammer the car, and in a moment moved away. Grady, emerging a moment later, said, "What the hell's all that about?"

"Beats me," Lucky said. "What's what about? You must be seeing stars or something at that certain time."

Grady tittered with them. "Guess I did see some stars," he said, in his best Ozark drawl. "Goddam, it's a sight, I'll tell ya." They all laughed with pleasure.

Next to last—someone elected last—full of odd anxiety and of odd desire, too, Dale took his turn. There was darkness and silence; the back seat area smelled of sex.

"Hi," Dale said.

There was no response.

"I said hi," Dale said.

"Holy shit, do it and get it over with!" the voice said.

He did it. At least he thought he did. His only hope, later, as his mind returned north at once and regret began to fill him, was that maybe, in fact, he had not done it. The target he sought in the dark—contact was made with an oily mass of hairy blubber—may not have been the primary target after all. Maybe it was an adjacent decoy. A trick perhaps on the greenhorn the girl knew him to be. The task completed itself in any case—on its own, it seemed—and at once there was the falling from wonder and the inward rush of regret. A moment later, as he returned his feet to the frozen ground—the air was cold now, where before it had been brisk—his distant mind, and his remote senses, too, opened entirely to let in cold air, and shivers, and guilt and shame enough to supply him down through the rest of his life. Oh, Zona, he thought.

"How was it?" someone asked as he returned to the gang.

"Nothing like a little nooky, hey, Dale?" someone said.

"Yeah," Dale said. "Nothing like it."

"Bet you kissed her, didn't you?" Chub said.

"Sure," Dale said. "Didn't you?"

Again they laughed with him, and Chub said no more.

Regret, guilt, shame, self-hate, whatever the emotions, they continued working double time. The big moment in the car, that climax of his life—it had just happened—and his hope now, as they started back, was that like horses he had ridden in childhood, and fighter planes he had flown, he still had a chance to do it for the first time.

He didn't, he knew.

At home, later, in the shower, he scrubbed and shampooed, to wash it away. The soap and hot water helped some, but not for long. The feeling had him, inside and out. In bed, in the dark, it did not lessen, but grew stronger. There was no satisfaction at all in having lost that which they spoke so often of losing, as if it were a tether which kept one from galloping on over the hill into manhood and good times. All he knew was endless regret over having misspent the one dollar he had saved and waited so long to spend. He hadn't wanted it to be like this, he thought. God, he hadn't wanted it to be like this at all. Oh, Zona.

During the night, Dale awakened several times, and knew each time that something was wrong. He might have stolen a car, or broken into a store, and known that he would be arrested in the morning and taken to the detention home.

At dawn, he sat on the side on his bed and held his head in his hands. He saw, there between his bare feet on the chilled linoleum, that one positive thing had happened during the night. His heartache over Zona Kaplan had changed. He no longer deserved her. The dream he had had of her was no longer his to dream. Heartache was a luxury.

The feeling of shame stayed with him on the bus, and in school. Sitting behind Zona, he hardly let himself glance her way. Touching her hair was out of the question now. The love he had known for her was not his anymore to expend. He had thrown it away. When homeroom ended, he moved, eyes averted, around the room to the door, and entering the hall, left her behind.

"You—you there, hillbilly!"

Dale looked back. He could not believe the man had called him that name like that and yet he knew he had. Did he think it was funny, or harmless, like calling someone pal or buddy? Dale was in the driveway and the garbage cans and lids, of course, were back by the curb. His face felt like it was burning.

"C'mere!" the man said. His voice was sharper this time and he glanced down again as Dale walked toward him, as if Dale were cowed now and at his command.

Dale did not know what he was. He was confused, he knew that, and he knew that he was either deeply upset or deeply angry. Nor did he know what he was going to do or say as he obeyed the man's orders; he knew that it was not exactly the man's orders which had him moving. He knew, too, that he was frightened in a way, was laced through with something like terror, even as he was hearing again what his father had said that time of Mr. Dusoe, of it being a time to show him what they were made of.

"You just walk right by those garbage cans!" the man was saying as Dale approached.

Dale needed a second. Then he said, "That's right," and then he said, "I'll walk anywhere," as he was unable for the moment to think of anything better to say. He looked the man in the eye.

The man saw something in him, Dale knew, still he said, "You people wouldn't be called hillbillies, and white trash, you know, if you took a—"

"Don't call me that," Dale said. "Don't call me that. Don't ever call me that. I'll beat your ass you call me that."

Dale felt livid, ferocious, even ready to cry, all of which he could see in the man's face—his eyes were like a mirror—as the man was backing up a step and getting himself more behind than beside the screen door. Quickly then, the man hooked the screen door—his hand came up, hooked the door, and he began to smile an odd smile. "Just listen to you," he said. "It's no wonder you people never get anywhere in this world—my God, just listen to you."

Dale reached his hand to the door handle and the man pulled back a little, and he said at once, as if it were his shirt or ear Dale had grabbed, "Get your hand off that door! Get your hand off that door right now!! Do you hear me?! Get your hand off that door!!"

Dale was pulling the door. He stood, glaring at the man, and not jerking the door but continuing to pull it toward him, putting his strength into it. "What're you calling me names for?" he said through the screen. "Why you doing that? I could beat you to a pulp. You know that? You don't scare me. I could beat you to a pulp if I wanted to."

"You get out of here!" the man said. "Get out of here!"

Dale kept looking at him and kept putting his strength into the door, and he could feel the hook begin to give, and knew it was coming free, or straightening. He kept his eyes on the man, and he continued to pull.

The man's eyes were wide. They glanced to the side, to the hook being separated, and back to Dale, and back again to the hook; he started to reach a hand to the hook and changed his mind, and as the screen door popped a little and came loose in Dale's hand, Mr. Barton had already jumped in behind the heavy wooden door and pushed it shut, and locked it.

Dale stood there. He was suddenly amused, but also frightened. He released the door handle, let the screen door close. He turned and walked on his way. He did not know what to think. What was the man doing inside the house? Was he doing anything? Was he calling the police? Dale walked on to the garage house, and he hoped that Mr. Barton, or his wife, was watching him from a window, to see that he was walking harmlessly away.

Only when he was inside, and in the midst of his excited fear, did he smile to himself and experience amazement over what had happened. He made a sound, trying to laugh, but could not feel any accompanying pleasure. He felt an urge to look in the mirror, perahps to see if he might ascertain whatever had happened. He did not look in the mirror. He moved into the kitchen instead, and looked through the window to the back of the landlord's house.

There was no sign of anything. The house stood there as usual. One hook undone, he thought.

• • •

On Sunday morning there was his father, standing in his bedroom doorway. He wore a three-piece suit, white shirt, and tie, and the color of whiskey was in his eyes. His teeth were stained that certain beige, too, within his crafty, intoxicated smile. Sunlight was glancing into the room in a knife blade behind him. Dale knew in his bones, even if he had been lying awake, that it was earlier than when he got up on school mornings.

"Spring has sprung!" his father said. "Came in overnight like a sweet sonofabitch. Warm air's out there right now!"

Maybe it was five-thirty. Dale rose to an elbow, looked at his father.

"Redsie, come on, let's take us a drive," his father said. "You won't ever see a more beautiful morning. Whatta ya say? Main thing—it's time you learned how to drive an automobile—and today is the day!"

Dale had been lying there thinking of the City League play-offs just ahead, and the idea cut through his cobwebs. His father was flushed and certainly he was drinking, still he was more happy than sodden. Early mornings were usually safe anyway; danger and uncertainty prevailed when it was dark or as the sun was going down, not when a new day was breaking.

Dale turned his legs out, sat up. "Okay," he said. "Okay."

"Now you are talking!" his father said. "Get dressed, Redsie—I'll fix you a bite to eat. I'll tell you. I am going to teach you how to drive so you won't ever forget it. Goddammit! Can't stand to see a man, woman either, who can't handle a car, who can't parallel park. Can't stand that kinda sappy person. Know what I mean? Let's roll it on out! *Ah-oohgah, oohgah!*" he added in train-whistle fashion, a pull there by his ear of the invisible cord. "*Ah-oohgah, oohgah!*" the train sounded again as it chugged away into the kitchen.

. . .

They were into the first week of March, the final, and biggest, basketball month of the year. The morning's sun today, though, was warm enough to belong to May. The sun was a ball of yellow-orange above the horizon and the sky was blue; the temperature seemed close to fifty and the sudden new air—as they went out into it, as Dale inhaled its warmth—was as special with promise as it seems to be only at age fifteen.

His father tossed him something—keys—and said, "All yours, Redsie. You're the captain. I might say a few things, but mostly I'm going to try to keep my mouth shut and let you teach yourself how to do it. Because—you know what? I'm gonna tell you something true. Anyone in this wide world ever had the head on their shoulders to do something, to do anything, it's you! Don't you forget it!"

Over the top of the car, looking at him, his father held a finger up as if in starting a new speech. "I've had a couple drinks, that may be true," he said. "I may be a little on the tipsy side. But I'm not giving you drunk talk. I know some things. And that's one thing I happen to know. You got a head on your shoulders. I've met lots of people who don't, I'll tell ya, and I've met a few who do, and you're one of those who do. I'm proud that you're my son!"

Dale slipped in behind the wheel. Building him up, telling him he had the stuff—it was something his father did when he drank and something, Dale knew, too, he took unto himself to a degree in spite of its alcohol content. Once, when a flare-up occurred over the subject, Dale had been completely surprised at his father's reaction. It was a clerk in a shoe store, a woman who was fitting new shoes to Dale's feet, and his father, to be sure, flush with drink, was into boozy nonsense about Dale being a good-looking young boy. The woman merely remarked, "Shouldn't fill a boy's head like that," and his father replied, after a moment and in the chilliest tone Dale had ever heard him use on anyone, "I'll take care of what I tell my son." And when they left, he added, "Don't pay any attention to some old cow like that. I don't care for that attitude. I've seen it a lot. People want to tear a young boy down is what they want to do. I don't know why. Maybe they want to keep them under their thumb or something. Not my boy, goddammit. I want my boy to think for himself. Always. Every time. Understand what I'm saying? I want you to be strong and I sure as hell want you to think for yourself. Fight 'em on the land and in the air. That's what a man is and does, and that's what I want you to do and be. That old cow, sonofabitch, screw her, she can go to hell is what she can do. I hate a person like that, I'll tell ya."

There was the steering wheel, the ignition. Dale was looking for the right key. He knew now, if he hadn't known before, that he would not mention the screen door incident to his father.

"Co-pilot to pilot," his father said. "First mate to captain. Going to tell you one more thing before I shut my mouth and let you take charge of this bomber."

Dale paused, smiled; he did not mind hearing his father's instructions and he sat looking ahead as he took in a brief lecture on "preparation behind the wheel." Adjusting rearview and side mirror, adjusting seat according to leg reach and arm reach, knowing where you're going and how you're going to get there.

"Fact, I'll tell you what I want you to do," his father said. "Right now. Before you even start the motor. I want you to get out of the car and walk around it. Get a feel for its size, its corners, what you'll be moving along the road. Get a feel for its width and length. It's glass and steel and rubber, Redsie, and if you want to be a first-rate driver, know that you are the heart and mind of such a piece of machinery. Know that it's only going to do what you tell it to do. Get out there now and feel it with your hands."

Reluctant, faintly suspicious—thinking, too, okay, keep him happy—Dale got back out of the car and walked around fenders, doors, trunk, grille, and bumpers. He even touched the warm metal a couple times, as instructed. And as he slipped back behind the wheel—he should have known, he thought—there was the sharp sweetish smell in the air, and he couldn't help laughing. "All that so you could take a drink?" he said.

His father laughed too, laughed some more. "Can't get away with nothing," he said. "You're getting too sharp for me. Anyway, crank her up and let's roll. I'm sure you know more than I think you do, about anything and everything, and I'm going to try, I am really going to try, I swear I am going to try to keep my mouth shut. Co-pilot to pilot. Taxi onto the runway. Let's get this show on the road!"

Feet fixed on brake and clutch, Dale turned the key. The motor fired and ran; he shifted one foot over to test the gas. *Vrhoom, vhroom!* went the engine. He raised his eyes to his father, who, watching him, winked.

"Redsie, you're a prize," his father said. "Swear to God you are. You're a prize I sure never deserved. I'm crazy about you. That's the truth. Long's you don't smash this up and get us both killed," he added. "Nah, heck," he added to this, reaching under the passenger seat to come up with a pint in a brown paper bag. "I'd be crazy about you even if you did that. What a way to go! Couldn't beat it, could you—taking the big dive together?"

Dale drove. He over- and underaccelerated some, ground the gears a few times, altogether lost power twice as the car lurched, as he moved it from their makeshift driveway beside the garage house, along the alley to quiet Sunday morning residential streets, to four-lane city streets, and back to two-lane streets. He managed stop signs, stop lights, occasional cars passing in the other direction and one backing out of a driveway without looking. His anxiety kept settling, however, and seemed in time to all but leave him. True to his word, his father sat still, sipped occasionally from his bottle, and let him teach himself, although Dale had a sense at times that his father was biting his lip to keep from lecturing.

"Good," his father said, as they pulled up to a red light. "Real good, Redsie, I mean it. You're doing it. I knew you could, and you are."

In another twenty-five or thirty minutes, parallel parking and down and uphill parking lessons behind them, they were cruising along a two-lane country road ten or fifteen miles outside the city, and his father was gazing through the windshield as an approximately relaxed passenger. Bringing up the bottle, tossing off a sip, letting it ride between his legs for a while and tossing off another, he seemed to be drifting away, to have left behind the idea that this was a driving lesson.

Dale was leaving the lesson behind too. Rarely getting out of the city—in the summer, usually, to go to a lake— he was experiencing a feeling of new beginnings existing here, as season and time of day were suggesting. He liked that the country was clean, liked especially the feeling that he was not known here, that there existed a remote possibility of recovering their dreams and chances. Basketball in a small town. What a star he'd be, he thought. He'd make all-county or something and everything would be different for both of them. Bill Wheeler and his son, Dale, the basketball player.

"Pop," Dale said, as he thought of it. "I met this guy. He said he knew you from down in Arkansas. Louis Treadway Junior is his name. Works at a diner near where I play City League."

"Louis Treadway. Oh, yes, I remember Louis Treadway. Louis Junior, and Louis Senior, too. They weren't ever actually my friends—they lived more out of than in town like I did. Where'd you say you met him?"

"At a diner. P and O Diner, on Corunna Street. He told

me—he said your father owned a store there, called 'Wheeler Dry Goods.' "

"Well, that's right, he did. That's what he told you?"

"He said—he said the name was chiseled there, in stone, and that it still is, because he was down there not long ago and saw it or something."

"Is that right?" his father said, coming back some, re-positioning himself in his seat. "I guess I thought that building would have been torn down by now. It's about like a name on a tombstone, you know."

"Well, not to me it isn't," Dale said. "Why don't you tell me stuff like that?" he added. "I'd like to know."

His father said nothing to this; he seemed, as Dale glanced his way, to be drifting again.

"He said it's used for a real estate office now," Dale said. When his father still did not respond, he said again, "Pop—how come you don't tell me stuff like that?"

His father looked his way. "I didn't mean not to," he said.

"It was all news to me," Dale said.

"Well, I'm sorry about that. You know it's all long ago and forgotten is what it is. But I'm sorry."

"But it's interesting to me," Dale said.

His father was uncapping the pint again, keeping it gripped and open when he had taken a sip. "Well, I guess I know that," he said. "I understand that. One of these days, Redsie, one of these days I'll tell you about that part of my life. Not that there's much to tell, or much I guess I like to tell, ya know?"

Dale drove along. His father, he could see to the side, was sitting staring away, still holding the opened pint in his hand. Dale imagined he was gazing toward Arkansas as it had been twenty-five years ago. He sipped again, kept staring away. Dale did not know what to say. He had thought of his father's father several times recently—it had occurred

to him that his father had *had* a father, and a mother, too—
and of the man's store, too, and had felt himself at times
to be all but a three-dimensional person. Maybe life in that
town—he imagined it to be compact, attractive, friendly—
maybe life there would be all that life here was not. Maybe
in a place like that a girl like Zona Kaplan wouldn't scratch
his name from her party list. He could see himself entering
their gym, too, their high school gym, a new boy in town,
putting on some moves which would have their eyes open,
would have them coming around to shake his hand. Fat
Frankie. That moment in his life would be erased, too,
even from his own mind.

"What happened to that store?" he asked his father.

His father took a second to refocus on him. "What's that?"
he said.

"What happened to that store?"

"That store got lost in the Depression."

"Is he still alive?" Dale said.

"Is who still alive?"

"Your father."

"No, son, my dad died a long time ago. So did my
mother, who was the dearest woman who ever lived."

"What—?" Dale said. "What were their names?"

Another pause followed, and Dale knew—as he kept
driving along the two-lane country road—that his father
was sitting staring ahead, gazing into something like eternity. Then he knew his father was looking his way and he
glanced to see one of his familiar, sly smiles. "I tell you
their names, will you let me off the hook for a while?" his
father said.

"I don't know," Dale said. "Why don't you ever want to
tell me anything?"

"That's not what it is. It's not that. What it is—well, it's
not anything I like talking about. Because—the truth is,
you see, I was a disappointment to my mother and my dad.

Even to their memory. Especially to my mother, because she believed in me and gave me every chance. It hurts to think of them. It makes me feel terrible to think of them, if you want to know the truth. It hurts just to speak their names."

Dale only glanced.

"I'll say this," his father said. "I'm sorry you never knew them. I'm sorry you didn't grow up where you could have known them as your grandparents. Before they died. Everything would have been different, if it had been like that. I'm sorry about the way things have worked out for you. I'm sorry your mother ran off like she did, although she was so young at the time I don't really blame her for anything anymore. Still, I'm sorry you've had to have the life you've had, living with me. Living like we do. It's something I'm sorry about every day. Every minute. It's too far gone and it's too big a thing for anyone to change now. Nothing can be done about it. That's why I'm sorry. I messed up a lot of things and you deserved better."

Dale gave no reply. If he spoke, he thought, he did not know how his words might come out or if his voice might break. He kept his hands on the wheel, looked ahead, drove on.

"Her name was Winifred," his father said then. "My mother. Her friends, my dad—everyone who knew her and liked her called her Winnie."

Dale kept driving. He liked the name. Winifred. He tightened the muscles in his face, because he knew his cheeks were trying to break. He kept driving, looked over his hands on the steering wheel to the pavement ahead. Winifred. He liked the name because his father liked it. He knew that, and he knew it over again as he drove along.

• • •

Saturday, as they dressed in the Walt Whitman locker room, Lucky came in and said, "This is it now—our last game of the regular season. Thursday—you all hear me—Thursday, after school, here, at three-thirty, we play the winner of the Lowell district. Stebbins Pharmacy."

"Thought we had to win today to get home court," Emmett said.

"We'll win," Grady said.

They won, easily. And on Thursday, when the bell rang to end the day at Whittier Junior High, Dale, ready, waiting as if to start a race, was immediately on the run, jacket and gym bag in hand. Two buses and several dashes of a hundred yards each; in the best of times, it was a forty-minute trip. His plan was to catch the first possible bus downtown, to sprint across the street and around the corner, to catch the first possible bus with CORUNNA ST in its glass brow, to dash across the street and into the Walt Whitman entrance and along its hallways, into the locker room, to undress and dress and stroll into the gym with his teammates.

As it happened, however, it was not the best of times. The first bus seemed to catch every possible red light, to find itself blocked out of making a green light by a car trying to park, to be driven by a man who had no sense of urgency whatsoever, one who chose to gab with a deboarding passenger while another green light turned red, who puttered along when he might have pressed the accelerator, who allowed every child and old person five minutes to cross the street, who found every opportunity to waste time. In the second bus, feeling crazed, Dale forced himself to stare at the floor, ordered himself—he was nearly successful—not to think of the game itself and how late he might be, forced himself into a numbness of not trying to change that which he could not change anyway.

At last, at Walt Whitman Junior High, Dale ran around in front of the bus and across the street and entered the school on the run, slipping like a broken-field runner through a handful of departing students. The visiting players would have been transported in cars by parents and coaches, and the three-thirty starting time was not unreasonable. As Dale tore into the locker room, however, it was silent and empty, and the caged clock over the door showed the time to be 3:31. His heart fell away.

He pulled his clothes off, jammed them into a locker, pulled on his uniform, his socks, hop-walked on one un-laced foot as he maneuvered his foot into the other sneaker and tied it, and hop-walked on that foot as he tied the other. At the door into the gym—a sudden, noisy, filled, excited space—he worked, entering, to tuck his orange jersey into his black shorts, moving across the floor to where his team-mates were huddling together before their bench just as the horn blared to indicate the start of the game.

His teammates took him in, in the midst of the noise and confusion. Their faces turned, they greeted him, said, "Hey, you made it, good, we were worried you wouldn't make it!" Lucky added, "Lloyd's starting but you come in at the first time-out; Lloyd, Little Wheel's coming in for you first time-out. This could be a tough game."

Sitting, Dale tried to catch his breath. The jump took place and the game was under way. Loosening his laces, Dale retightened and retied them, quickly, firmly. He was ready, and, at once, it seemed, a whistle blew and there was Lloyd coming off the floor. On his feet, Dale moved toward the others. From the stands, nearby, someone called, "Who's that?" and someone said, "Hey, Lucky, who's number five?"

Dale received an inbounds pass from Emmett Booker, the other guard, to begin moving the ball downcourt. It was a game. Stebbins Pharmacy was a real team, and at once it was a real game. Dale had known this the moment he walked into the midst of the players. The crowd of spectators, the thrill and excitement were there. And at once, feeling suddenly excited and aggressive, taking them all by surprise, including himself, he was firing a long, high sixty-foot pass all the way to Chub near the basket at the other end. Chub leapt to whip the ball out of the air and, on a dribble and pivot, laid it in off the board, to an explosive roar from the crowd. Dale heard Lucky call to one side, moving back downcourt, *"That's who number five is!"* And he waved a fist to Dale, and called, as did both Grady and Chub, "Great pass! Great pass! Keep it up! These guys are good!"

"Zone?" Dale asked at mid-court. "We're playing zone?"

"Yeah, zone, let's play zone," Lucky said.

The Little M's played zone. It was their method, their game plan. On other teams in Dale's experience there would have been a practice and team meeting the day or night before a big game, probably several practices and chalk talks over several days, and the coach would have laid out, harangued endlessly upon their game plan, their opening strategy, their fast-break, full-court, and half-court pickups, their rotations, even, for the captains, their use of time-outs. Only in Summer League, outdoors under the lights and the players self-coached on the spot, would strategy be both spontaneous and sometimes brilliant, too, and excitement of that spontaneous kind was in Dale now as the other team was approaching with the ball. It was a greater charge not being coached, not having someone telling you everything to do and being angry all the time it wasn't being done that way.

Nor had Stebbins Pharmacy played a team of their caliber; this was clear when they attempted to move the ball along the side and it was slapped out of bounds by Grady Devlin. And when Dale jumped, gave all possible acceleration, tapped away still another pass, ran to recover the ball, dribbled twice, and laid it in over the lip of the rim, to another explosion from the crowd—nothing had ever exhilarated him like such approval from a crowd—he knew he was flying high, flying faster, harder, quicker than in any game in some time.

The playoffs. One-game elimination. He had almost forgotten how exciting it was to attempt to move on one game at a time. And as he heard his number called from the stands, as if he had forgotten it, misplaced it, he took in like new air the wonderful thrill and desire to play and win, the possession of desire and confidence, the satisfaction that was a game.

The Little M's lost the lead and got it back and would lead throughout, if only by three or four points. Still it was a true game all the way, and when the final horn sounded, when the players of Stebbins Pharmacy were left stunned in their defeat, their elimination, the Little M's carried their excitement into the locker room, and into the gang shower, and, as spring awaited them outdoors and the locker room seemed stifling with heat and stale air, as it had not when snow had filled gray skies, they carried the feeling outside and across the street to the P & O Diner, pushing around and joking as they waited for Lucky to come along with news of the next game in the playoff ladder.

Dale knew there was a chance it would be the Michigan Truckers, but he tried not to think about it. He had not felt so good in weeks, or months, it seemed, and for the first time, he joined without reservation the noise and horseplay of his teammates as they pushed around and joked and laughed there on the sidewalk.

"Wheeler, you're not a bad player," Chub remarked in the midst of the melee. "I'll tell you the truth. I didn't think Lucky shoulda signed you up like he did, but you can sure play the game, man, and without you we might not a won today."

Embarrassed, pleased, Dale laughed in excess as Chub

added, "Besides that, you're a hillbilly redneck just like the rest of us, so it's okay he signed you up."

There was Lucky, coming on the run across the street. Then he slowed down, and Dale tried in a way not to hear what was coming. "Thursday, three-thirty," Lucky said. "Team called Michigan Truckers. Your guys, Dale. At your school."

Dale had felt it, but had not quite let it in, and it still came to him as a shock. His school. The Truckers.

"What do you think, Dale—can we beat those bastards?" Grady Devlin said.

"I don't know," Dale said. "They got a good team."

"We can't beat 'em in the gym," Chub said, "we'll do it in the parking lot."

He wasn't quite joking, and Grady, not joking either, added, "We could do both, if we wanted."

"Winner plays downtown Saturday, for the city," Lucky said.

"For the city?" Emmett said.

"City championship," Lucky said. "That's what it's all about."

Dale's heart felt gripped and weighted. He had not let himself imagine this, or if he had, had seen it as just another dream. Here it was. And at once it was inside him, filling him with fear and excitement and something like unexpected anger and energy. To play at his school, in his gym, against the Michigan Truckers. To dress in his locker room, in the company of his new teammates, to go into the gym, onto the floor, in the visiting uniform. At once he had a feeling of wanting to fight, and of wanting to do it right now.

Orange and black. Take no flak.

The Little M's.

What's that M stand for? the students at his school would say. Rednecks from Little Missouri. Southerners up north to work in the factories. Hillbillies who live in those little square houses, who speak with those funny twangs and drawls.

"We can beat 'em!" Dale said.

"Goddam right we can!" Lucky said.

"We'll kick ass!" Chub said.

"We got to!" Dale said. "We got to! I mean it!"

Dale still wanted to do it then, in that moment. He was ready. He was unbeatable. He had that feeling. But they had to wait a week, and now they had to go home and go on with school and life until the day arrived. Emmett, the first to leave, said, "See you at your school on Thursday, Dale," and walked away.

As the others dispersed and Dale went back across the street to catch the first leg of his bus trip home, he found he was too excited still, too nervous, to stand at a bus stop and wait. He walked on, and walked on, to catch the bus at the next corner, and then at the next, and then at the next.

The beating of Sonny Joe Dillard. He had never thought before of the beating of Sonny Joe Dillard. He may never have thought that Sonny Joe could be beaten. He thought of it now, though, and the idea was taking off in his mind. He walked on. There was one person who could beat Sonny Joe, he thought and knew. One person. It was the person whose heart knew the desire, whose heart could hear the call.

Dale kept walking. He knew who the person was, for sure. It was the person they had decided to cheat and steal from, and to cast aside, the person the girls of his school did not invite to their party while they invited those who had stolen his dream. It was the person who was walking this sidewalk now, who was nearly out of his mind with all that he knew.

PART
THREE

M onday in school a boy Dale hardly knew mentioned the forthcoming game. Dale was turning from a drinking fountain when the boy said, "Hey, good luck in the game this week."

"Thanks," Dale said.

He was pleased, but only for a moment. It came to him that the boy had to think he played for the Truckers. That's what it was. Did anyone, even the Truckers, know that he had joined a team in another district? He hadn't told anyone. Had he? He couldn't remember telling anyone.

As usual, in his movements throughout the school, he passed the Truckers' players. He nodded, said "Hi," as always, and so did they. Business as usual. It may have been Wednesday when he noticed, coming from Hal Doyle, the faintest smile of derision.

The boy's faint smile hung around in Dale's mind. Complete confidence, Dale thought. The little smile said the Truckers were altogether confident. It also seemed to say that it was him they had in their sights. It said, too, Dale thought—otherwise they wouldn't have been so cocksure— we have Sonny Joe Dillard on our side. A thirst for blood, he thought. That's what it was. A thirst for the blood running in his arms and legs swinging along with him as he walked.

No surprise, Dale thought. Of course they'd want to defeat his team, and mainly defeat him, badly, to justify their crime. For he was the one who would call up disloyalty, if it was in them to be called up. He was the one they'd have to hate. Not the Little M's. They were merely another enemy team. He would be inside them, a bug in their team conscience. They wouldn't necessarily know it, he thought, because they hardly ever thought of things anyway. But something within them would know it. And Mr. Bothner and stupid Burkebutt would know it, if only in their stupid bones. They would want to destroy his ass. That was the word in the faint curve-smile of Hal Doyle's lips. Destroy Wheeler's ass. What they wouldn't know, he thought, was that while they wanted to destroy his, he wanted to obliterate theirs.

Did other students know that he would come out in orange and black? Was it news at all that on Thursday Dale Wheeler would play *against* the team identified with his school? What of the girls—did they know? Did it mean anything to any of them? To Zona Kaplan? Going along a hallway on the second floor, he saw two girls who, glancing at him, put their heads together, whispered and tittered and glanced back. Were those smiles of derision? Or had his imagination fallen prey to the athlete's vanity cited so often by girls? "They're so conceited!" they said, and "They think they're such hot stuff!" even as hot-stuff boys were the ones the girls seemed always to pursue. Sonny Joe Dillard, everyone said, could have any girl he wanted.

Each moment in school passed strangely for Dale. Only when he was away from the long brick building, riding buses or at home, did the world seem nearly ordinary again.

Wednesday, as school ended, any doubt he had of what the Truckers knew was removed. Leaving school, walking along with his books and gym bag, Sonny Joe appeared beside him.

"Dale, how's it going?" Joe said.

"Okay. How you doing?"

Joe did not say. At the sidewalk intersection before the school, where Dale usually turned right and Joe usually turned left, Joe said, "Which way you going?"

"This way," Dale said. Other students were gathering, waiting to cross, lining up for buses. Joe continued walking with him, leaving the mob of students behind.

"I don't know how to say this," Joe began. "Listen, I want you to know I'm sorry, you know, we're playing our last game against each other. You know . . . after all the games we played here. Comes down to our last game and we're playing our last game against each other."

"Yeah," Dale said.

"We've always been teammates and friends," Joe said. "My dad asked me the other day how come you weren't on the team now and when I told him he said it didn't sound real fair that you were left off."

"Yeah, well, that's all long gone now," Dale said.

"What's long gone?"

"Everything's long gone. Nobody cares what's fair. You guys all went along with the Bothners, and Burkebutt was too chicken to stand up to them. It's too late to talk about what's fair."

"Gee, I'm sorry," Joe said. "I didn't know you felt like that."

"Give me a break. You're the one who told me! Oh, forget it," Dale added, to keep himself from spinning out of control yet again.

"Anyway, I'm just sorry we're going to play our last game against each other, that's all," Joe said. He had stopped, was preparing to turn back the other way.

"Just another polka," Dale said.

"Of course we're going to whip your ass," Joe said, showing his smile—one Dale knew well—of pure confidence.

"Well, we'll see what happens," Dale said.

Dale started away, but after a step Joe called after him. "Dale, I know you wanted to be on the team, but I didn't know you were so mad about it. I know you sort of got screwed."

Dale was looking back. "No sort of about it," he said.

To Dale's surprise—as he felt himself going to pieces again within—Joe, ten or twelve feet away, was smiling. "Anyway, it'll be your last game of the year and our next-to-last," Joe said. "Come on downtown on Saturday—see the Michigan Truckers win the City."

"Thought you went to Sunday School," Dale managed to say. "Thought they taught you not to profane your neighbor."

Joe laughed. "What do you know about profaning your neighbor?" he said.

"I don't know, but I used to be your neighbor and you just did it," Dale said as Miss Turbush flashed into his mind and he knew that he was losing it again.

"You're not my neighbor."

"I was," Dale said. "I'm not anymore." This time Dale turned away, because he had to.

"Hey, Dale, sorry," Joe called behind him.

Dale kept walking, as his eyes were blurring. You're not sorry, he cried to himself. You're not. Nobody is. Nobody ever said anything. You all let me get dumped off the team and nobody ever said anything. I'm gonna beat your ass on Thursday! he added to himself as the blurring continued. I'm gonna beat you, you fucker asshole sonofabitch!

Dale walked all the way home. His eyes had dried in time, but he had no feeling to ride the bus, or to hurry either. Moving as slowly as a lost five-year-old who is bewildered by all things, confused even by the sky and by the naked trees, he turned at last into the alley, on the last leg of the four-mile walk. He glanced up, continuing his wandering pace, and he began to know that something else was wrong even before he knew what it was.

His father's car was there. The green Chevy was in its place next to the small house. Dale's heart sank. Booze. Another drunken babe. Sloppy words and sentimental music. He stopped walking and aloud, faintly, he said, "Jesus, not now, not today." Well, he had to check. He had, at least, to get clean socks for tomorrow's game.

There was silence over all as he drew closer. No sounds, no signs. It could be anything, he realized as he moved past the dusty side of the car to the door into the garage house. With his father, it could be anything. Trying the doorknob, not using his key, he opened the door.

There was no music playing and a light was on in the kitchen. There had been those times, of course, long ago, when he had come home to the welcome surprise of his father's company, and he tried to think of them now.

"Pop?" he said, in a most ordinary way.

"In here," his father said, and in the next second he appeared from the stove end of the kitchenette. His left arm was before him in a white sling. Smiling, he appeared sober.

"What's *that!?*" Dale said. "What happened?" What he felt, though, was a wave of relief that his father was sober, and alive.

"Lost part of a finger," his father said. "They doped me up and sent me home."

"Lost part of a *finger?*"

"Sheet metal machine took it right off. Just like that."

"It did?" Dale said. "Really?"

His father's left forefinger and much of his hand, peeking from the sling, was wrapped in tape and gauze. In spite of all the tape, the forefinger was shorter than its pink, exposed neighbor. His father was showing it to him. "Right there," he said. "Took one knuckle, just missed the other."

"Does it hurt?"

"Oh, yes and no," his father said. "Gave me kind of a shock when it happened. Then it didn't hurt so much for a while. Then it began to hurt quite a bit. Right now they got me so fulla morphine it's not bad at all. What really hurts," he added, a sparkle seeming to flash in his eye, "is the piece that got away. Landed in the middle of those metal shavings, took off running, and nobody ever could find it."

"The part—took off running?" Dale said.

"Was a sizable chunk of your old dad, son. Coulda used some morphine, 'cause it hurt too. I think it was worried about getting stepped on."

"I see," Dale said.

"Ran like a head with its chicken cut off."

Dale smiled at this, laughed. "You been waiting to say that, haven't you," he said. He couldn't help laughing some more as he said, "A head with its chicken cut off. That's pretty funny. Is that what morphine does to you? Makes you into a comedian? That's what I heard it does."

His father was giggling so much his eyes were glossy. "They got me feeling a little silly, it's true," he said. "Problem is, I'm not supposed to drink any hard stuff. Has me in a hell of a fix here, I'll tell ya. I'm SOBER as a goddammed judge! Can you believe that?"

"You don't feel anything at all?" Dale said. "In your finger, I mean."

"Feeling no pain, son. It's like you always hear. You feel the part that's not there. Like when your nose tickles and you can't scratch it. End of that finger feels like that and what I want to do is scratch it against something, which I can't do, a course, because it's not there to scratch."

Dale smiled, as his father added, "Truth is, son, its one of those situations where you go along with your head more or less in the clouds, then something like this happens and lets you know how close you are to the other side of things."

Dale nodded, smiling still.

"The way I figure," his father said. "That one finger joint is gone on ahead like a scout. Gonna check things out with the angels and report back. No, I'm just kidding. What I was really thinking. I mean, I know it's the morphine getting ideas in my head, but what I saw was that piece of finger heading back to Arkansas, like you were asking about the other day. It would work like a seed, you see, and sprout a new me down there. And a new you. And what we'd do is start life all over again, and do it right this time."

Dale only nodded; he did not know what to say.

In another moment, when Dale still had not responded, his father said, "Anyway—you hungry, son? It's about dinner time, isn't it? We work together here, we can fix us up a little bite to eat."

Should he invite his father to the game tomorrow? Dale was close to doing so, even as something within kept warning him against it. If his father did not have to go to work, Dale thought, he could make it easily. Dale was close to doing it, to saying something—thinking maybe it would give him luck in some way—at the same time that images of the game of two years ago came to mind. He thought, too, that he might choke and play badly if his father was there, maybe because he was sober.

They sat at the table to eat, and Dale still did not raise the subject, however much he seemed to be waiting for the right moment. To his surprise then—it had to be the morphine—his father said he was going to bed, said he needed a good night's sleep, and Dale let him go without mentioning what was on his mind.

He wasn't going to ask him, Dale admitted to himself as

he cleaned up the dishes. He felt selfish about it, but he knew he wasn't going to do it. Downtown, for the City, but not to his school for this game.

Dale came to himself sitting on the couch, staring away. He wasn't sure where his thoughts had been, only that he had been on a trip somewhere, into something. Basketball. Had he given his heart to basketball? It seemed that he had. Was that what a real athlete did—give his heart to his sport? Had all the good players given their hearts? Dale took a breath and got to his feet. It was time, he knew, to take the first step on that certain road: getting his uniform ready for tomorrow's game.

Preparation the night before was something he had developed into a ritual for big games. A year ago, two years ago, he began to associate winning and losing, having a good game or having a poor game, with details of preparation from the night before. Big games might not be won in a dirty uniform. The reason for a loss would be obvious; not missed shots or bad passes, but smelly jersey and crusty socks, from which missed shots and bad passes derived. Clean shoelaces could make the difference in a big game, and an advantage might be gained, too, from removing staple and label from new socks, even as new socks were not something he could always afford. Being ready, more than ready, was the key.

The question playing in the back of his mind: Would special preparation work for this game? Would it make any difference at all? Should he defy preparation, turn his back on it, tell it to get lost, wear dirty socks and turn the tables on fate itself? Be cool, and not a fool?

Socks, jock, black shorts, orange jersey. He decided to go with what was most reliable; he'd wash them all. Still there was a lingering question: His shoelaces? Would it help this time, or not? Would it be exactly the right thing? Or might it be the wrong thing? Might dirty laces be the token defiance which would carry them to victory?

Laces question on hold, he sloshed jersey, shorts, and jock into a plugged sink of soapy water in the bathroom. He had plenty of clean white wool socks, and he identified and laid out the thickest two on his bed, next to a clean towel, and removed their crusty counterparts from his gym bag.

Well, he felt okay, he thought. One thing about his father losing part of a finger, it had taken his mind off the things that had been eating at him when he turned into the alley a few hours ago. Now here he was and time had slipped away, was slipping away still as he sloshed the items in the sink in clean water.

His father had been right to call it stealing, Dale thought yet again. Mr. Von Bothner entered the school clearly intending to steal a team for his sons, managed Coach Burke without any trouble whatsoever—managing Coach Burke must have made him smile—and left with a team which had at its center the best player of his age in the city, maybe in the state, one of the best players in the city's history. Mr. Bothner must have felt like a real whiz, Dale thought, when he arrived home with the present to give to his sons, even if what he was giving them belonged to someone else.

The Blue Arrows, Dale thought. His dream. He had worked for them for two years, and dreamed of them day and night. Winning the City was the first big-deal dream he had ever had, and Mr. Bothner had simply stepped in and carried it away to give to his sons.

Well, forget it, Dale said to himself as he started wringing the rinsed items, shaking them out, draping them over hangers to hang above the space heater in the living room. Forget it. Let it go, he told himself as the old hurt was coming up once more in his throat. Stop it from showing up in your mind. He found he could not stop it, though. It refused to just leave, and there he was leaning in between the shower stall and toilet, looking to the floor, sighing once more against the impossibility of things.

Well, he'd go for it, he said to himself at last, straightening up. He'd try everything.

In his bedroom, he pulled his white sneakers from his gym bag. He'd made his decision, and back in the bathroom, he unstripped the dirty laces. Wildly. Wadding and rubbing them into a bar of soap until they were slimy, he scrubbed them together. He'd try everything, he thought. He'd try anything and everything he could think of. Orange and black, take no flak. Always show up and always fight back.

In the morning, in homeroom, Zona Kaplan turned to him and said, "You're playing against your own *school?!?*"

Dale was confused. How could anything or anyone be so unfair? She had gone over to their side, and now she was accusing *him* of not being loyal. Still, he did not know what to say.

In a moment, he leaned ahead; his voice trembled as he said, at last, "I told you they wouldn't let me be on the team. Mr. Bothner just took over the team and wouldn't let me be on it. It was because I'm better than his dumb son! Even Coach Burke told me that!"

"What's that supposed to mean?" she said.

"Oh, God, what do you think it's supposed to mean?! Jesus, just forget it!" Nonetheless, Dale leaned ahead and added, "It means just what I said! Mr. Bothner stole the team! He stole it and he didn't want me on it because he knows I'm better than his stupid son! That's what it means!"

"Stupid son? Which son?"

"Both!" Dale said.

"You don't even know them," she said.

"I don't want to, either."

"I happen to think they're very nice," she said. "Both of them. They're not stupid, that's for sure, and they're a lot *cuter* than lots of people I know who go around calling people names." She returned her head to the front.

Dale sat there. Cuter? *Cuter?* There was her hair, her neck. Against his better judgment, not knowing where he was going, he leaned toward her again and said, "If what you think is they're cute, then you're the one who's stupid!"

In a moment, from a higher angle, she swiveled her neck to find him again. "You've never met them," she told him. "And you know all of what they're like. Excuse me if that is not the most intelligent thing I've ever heard!" On the merest pause, she turned to the front yet again.

Dale no longer liked her. Liking her had left him. How could he have liked her so much? "You just like them because you think they're rich or something," he said.

She sat there, made no move to look his way. He did not know if she was hurt or angry, and he kept expecting her to look around and say something even stronger.

She simply sat there, however, and in a moment, feeling sorry for what he had said, he leaned toward her neck, again not knowing what he was going to say. "You say I'm not loyal or something, but you're the one who's not loyal," he said in a confused voice. "You didn't invite me to that party and you invited them, and you lied, too, because you acted like you had invited me and you knew you hadn't. I always used to like you but I don't anymore and I used to really love you."

Nor did Zona Kaplan respond to this. She did not move. Dale looked to the side, to the windows. Others came into the room, and only in time, as Miss Turbush started the business of homeroom, did he begin to shed his crazed emotion. Had other students heard what he said? He studied the surface of his desk. Oh, none of it matters, he told himself. Nothing matters. He stared into himself, and in time, when the bell rang, he got to his feet and looked ahead as he walked from the room.

The shoelaces, in their staircase braid in his sneakers, were still damp. He positioned his P. F. Flyers on the bench, to give the laces some air. He did not want extra weight on his feet, not even the vague addition of moisture in the white laces.

The first to arrive, he sat on the bench before his locker and continued his careful undressing and dressing for the game. Dressed—still early, still the only one in the locker room—he placed one foot at a time on the bench to pull the damp laces tight, to tie them firmly at the top. It was the last detail. He was ready. And as he stood upright, he heard others enter and from the location and voices knew them to be his one-time friends and teammates, who were now the Michigan Truckers.

Orange and black. He looked down over himself. An orange and black commando, he thought. One, you dumb jerks, who will strike at dawn.

Dale sat on the bench again, to relax some if he could, to simply sit and think for a minute. He thought of little, it seemed, in this moment, and he thought of everything. He envisioned things. He envisioned school, he even envisioned the planet—the globe in the second-floor Reference Room—tumbling through the universe as countless persons like specks of dust died and were born, as Mr. Wright had once described it. Dale took in his orange jersey again, too, and its number 5, front and back in different

sizes. Zona Kaplan's sheen of black hair also came to mind, until he said to himself that he had to let her go now, he had to forget Zona Kaplan forever.

Girls had never quite liked him, he knew, because he wasn't real good-looking. His nose had been sort of flattened by football cleats on the feet of a tub from St. Michael's he had once tried to tackle—the bridge of his nose had probably been broken, and never set or fixed—and his teeth were also sort of crooked on one side. Well, they were crooked, no sort of about it. He wasn't cute, that was for sure. In fact, he was sort of homely. Still, when the time came to do the job, he knew in his heart that he was someone who could do it. It was what he knew. If the wind blew and the building collapsed, he would not give in to fear and he would know what to do. It was something he had known for a couple years now. He wasn't cute, but when the boys who were cute were unable and frightened, he was the one to whom they would turn to save them. And it was what he would do. It was what he was here for, tumbling through the universe, if his nose was bent and his teeth were crooked or not.

New voices startled him. It was more of the enemy—the main body—entering in a gang. There was Sonny Joe's voice, Hal Doyle's, others. They moved into their regular place a couple aisles over, opened lockers, exchanged remarks, sang lines, made boy noises, clucks, grunts, yelps. Well, it's real, Dale thought. The game is real now. It's happening. In a little while he'd go out on the floor in his orange and black uniform and play against his former teammates. Startled, sensing that someone had appeared at the end of his aisle, he looked over to see Hal Doyle standing there sock-footed, unbuttoning his shirt, that certain smile on his face.

"Wheels, where's your team?"

"They'll be here," Dale said. "Where's yours?"

"What're you doing, sitting there praying?" the boy said as, on a giggle, he moved away.

Dale sat brooding, wishing he had said something else, or had called something out after the boy. He stood up, but only stood with his muscles tensed.

His arms and legs, he realized, were like loaded guns. It was what he had wanted, how he had planned it—to be dressed before the Truckers were dressed, and before his own teammates arrived. He was doing it right, was on top of it, was playing his game. He was ready.

At once, in the midst of new sounds of arrival, a voice bellowed into the locker room, "HULLO, ASSHOLES— LITTLE M'S IS HERE!"

Lucky! Dale was thrilled, called to battle, so proud all at once of his new friends that his breath seemed to catch. *These* were his friends now, his pals, his teammates! *See,* he imagined saying to the Truckers. *See!* Take that, you bunch of dinks! He stood up to meet the Little M's; he felt suddenly like a nervous host whose guests—a gang of them—were going to see where he lived for the first time.

They turned into his aisle and Dale was shocked. Lucky, Grady, Chub, a couple of the others, wore dark blue double-breasted overcoats over dress shirts without neckties. Their slacks, pegged, touched upon thick-soled glossy Jarmans. They looked older, smarter, powerful. They looked like a gang of hoods.

"Watch your language, hillbilly!" one of the Truckers— Hal Doyle trying to keep his voice deep, Dale thought— called out.

The Little M's, filling Dale's aisle, were laughing, hooting, tossing bags, opening locker doors, unbuttoning coats. "What language you talking about, shithead fuckface asshole?" Chub called back over the lockers, his challenge ominous, where Lucky's had been a little funny.

This silenced the Truckers for a moment, until someone

called back, "We'll show you hillbillies what language on the court."

"Goodness me, we have interrupted youth fellowship," Grady Devlin said in turn, his white teeth flashing.

The Little M's laughed. They were all high, it was clear. Lucky bellowed, "WE GOT A SECRET WEAPON— LITTLE WHEEL GONNA RUN OVER YOUR RICH SNOB FAT ASSES!!"

Lucky, sitting on the bench as he called this, removing a shoe, winked at Dale, and Dale experienced an added charge of affection and admiration for him and for them all. Yes, he had teammates, was on a team. He wasn't alone.

"He's a hillbilly too!" Hal Doyle called back. "That's why he's not on our team."

"Go fuck yourself, pal," Grady said, unlike himself this time and not smiling. Getting to his feet, he said to Dale, "Don't worry—they wanna fight, that's one thing we sure as hell know how to do."

"I'm not worried," Dale said.

"We playing in the big gym?" Chub asked.

"I hope so," Dale said. "We can beat them in the big gym."

"How's that?" Lucky asked.

"I don't know," Dale said. "I just know we can."

"How come this school's so *clean?*" Lloyd asked.

They all laughed.

"Listen," Lucky said. "Listen, Dale, you be captain today. Everybody—Little Wheel's captain today, in his school."

"What about those Bothner brothers?" Grady asked. "They any good?"

"I guess they're not bad," Dale said. "The older one, who plays forward, is real big, I guess, and I hear he's not bad. Only he's a little slow, and hasn't played that much, not against good teams, and he's sort of clumsy. The younger brother—he's their passing guard—what I hear about him is he's a little prick with ears. The older one is nice is what everyone says, and the younger one is a little prick."

"Can he play though?" Chub said.

"I guess so," Dale said. "I've heard he can—I've never seen either one of them."

"We got our work cut out for us," Grady said.

"For sure," Dale said. "Sonny Joe scores about half or two thirds of their points, so he's the one we have to stop."

"I'll stop him," Chub said. "Don't worry."

In the next moment, it seemed, everyone was dressed and ready and shaking out, closing locker doors, fixing locks.

"Let's huddle," Lucky said.

They gathered around.

"Don't think we can't beat these guys," Dale said within their circle. "I know we can."

"Don't anybody play scared now," Lucky said. "Make them play scared. Make them play our game. You get a chance, throw a goddam elbow, stomp a toe. These guys are gonna be good, I know—let's put a scare into their rich snob fat asses as soon as we can. Okay, Little M's—let's go out there and do the deed!"

Dale checked his laces, as if they weren't tight. Goose bumps ran over his arms and thighs. He followed along. He wanted to enter last, he realized, or not at all.

Moving into the tunnel, they pulled up as they approached the doorway. Before them was the full sweep of the gym. Dale, in the middle, paused with the others; his heart seemed to be fluttering. The lion's den, a boxing ring, courtroom, cathedral; it was all things to him, even as a thought ran crazily through his mind of Miss Turbush being there—he had never seen her at a game—ordering him off the floor like a second grader for being inappropriately dressed.

Bleachers were in place on both sides of the gym, and between naked shoulders before him Dale could see the making of a crowd of spectators, moving upon, sitting upon the dozens of rows of blond wooden planks. His stomach seemed to churn with anxiety, as if on the edge of being sick. They were the planks through which his father had lost leg and bottle.

"Let's go," someone said, and they were moving from the tunnel, entering the vast space. Afternoon March light from the row of windows on one side filled the gym, high-lighting the lacquered floor. Dale's ears buzzed.

In ragged file, they loped under the nearest basket and pulled up to wait. The white backboards on either end had been lowered and locked into place. A single ripple-response was greeting them, followed by scattered hoots, boos, hisses, perhaps two sets of hands applauding. The enemy had appeared, in orange and black. Dale's ears still buzzed.

"You could eat scrambled eggs off this floor," Lloyd said.

"I'll get some balls," Dale said, going on to the scorer's table at the side while his teammates held up near the center. Before him were two officials in their black-and-white striped shirts. Two other men—scorekeeper and time-keeper—sat behind the long folding table, and, standing at the end of the bench on the near side, the school's usual home bench and home side, Coach Burke was in conversation with another man, perhaps a parent or a league of-ficial. The two of them, in suits and ties, seemed, like the others, not to have noticed his presence.

To the men at the table, Dale said, "We need a couple balls to warm up with." His voice sounded like it belonged to someone else.

The two men looked around, to see if balls were available, and one of the officials, holding a new leather ball at his side, turned and said, "This is a game ball—we have two new game balls—but you can't use these."

"Your team didn't bring warm-up balls?" Coach Burke said, looking his way.

"No," Dale said.

"You should have," Coach Burke said.

"School always provides them," Dale said.

"Not for City League," Coach Burke said. "You know that."

"They always have," Dale said.

"Read the rule book," Coach Burke said.

"We can't use balls to warm up with?" Dale said.

"Host school provides balls for regular season games," Coach Burke said. "That's the arrangement. For play-offs you're supposed to bring balls from your host school."

"We didn't," Dale said. "Nobody ever does that."

In that moment, to a sudden roar from the growing crowd, the Michigan Truckers came trotting down the center of the floor, their red-and-silver uniforms glistening. The first five of the ten or twelve players were dribbling new, pebbly leather balls. At the far end they moved nonstop into a passing-running drill—quick fingertip passes—which appeared so polished and professional it drew not only the astonished stares of the Little M's standing out there, but spontaneous added applause from the gathering crowd.

Appearing behind them, dressed in suit, white shirt, and tie, clipboard at his side in one hand, was the giant-sized, silver-haired, one-time Fort Wayne Zollner Piston, Mr. Von Bothner, and he, too, seemed to draw applause, on presence alone. He raised a hand as he walked, and still more applause rang out. The school was proud. Burkebutt, Dale noticed, was clapping wildly. There was a smile on his face which wouldn't quit.

Into the end of this, Dale said something about borrowing balls for warm-up, but did not hear any reply as everyone along the side kept watching the Michigan Truckers' fluid procession. Dale looked over to watch it himself. Then he said, more clearly, "We can't borrow some balls?" and the official looked at him, not knowing what to say or to do.

Dale stepped over to his teammates (he heard someone shout, "Hey, Wheeler, you traitor!"), to whom he said, "They won't let us borrow any warm-up balls; we were supposed to bring our own."

Another well-rehearsed drill was under way at the far end. Dale stood and watched with the others, saw the new leather balls going one after another off the board and through hoop and net.

Confused—everything seemed wrong and lost already—Dale walked over once more to the officials standing before the folding table at the side. The eyes of the two men in black and white, and those of the others standing there, were still on the Truckers at the end, running yet another professional-style drill.

"Who's the main ref?" Dale said.

No one replied, or looked his way.

Dale stood there. "Who's the main ref?" he said, a little more loudly, into the gym's swollen din.

The official holding the ball at his side looked his way. "I'm head official today," he said. "Are you team captain? If you're not team captain, send over your team captain and I'll answer any question he has. This game is going to start in about three minutes."

"I'm team captain," Dale said.

"Okay, what's the problem?"

"The problem is we don't have any balls to warm up with," Dale said.

The man opened his free hand, to say he was sorry, there was nothing he could do about it.

"They get five balls to warm up with and we don't get any?" Dale said.

"Coach—Coach Burke," the official said. "Can't you let these kids borrow a couple balls?"

Coach Burke had turned his head. "Host school is *not* obligated to furnish warm-up balls during play-offs," he said. "It's in the rule book. In City League, during play-offs, host school is a neutral site. I thought I just said that."

"Nobody ever brings balls," Dale said, an unwelcomed strain in his voice.

The faintest smile came to Coach Burke's face. "This young man is a troublemaker," he said to the official.

Dale did not know what to say. Nor did the official seem to have a response and, mission accomplished, Coach Burke looked away again to watch the Truckers continue their impressive routine. Almost at once, in obvious pleasure with the scene out on the floor, a new smile was on Coach Burke's face, the pest at his side apparently forgotten.

The official also turned his attention back to the Truckers' warm-up. Dale looked from one to the other; the smile on Coach Burke's face, in profile, reminded him, he realized, of the smile on the landlord's face before he had straightened his screen door hook.

He did not know what to say or do. He walked toward his teammates, who, like everyone else, stood watching the Truckers' ongoing performance. "We're going to start in about one minute," the official called behind him.

Dale glanced back, to acknowledge, but the official was already leaning down to say something to the men seated at the scorer's table. Dale went on to his teammates. He wanted to say something reassuring to them, but for the moment felt too confused, too embarrassed, to say anything. Then he heard himself say, "It's going to start in about a minute."

His teammates more or less nodded; their attention remained drawn to the drill being executed so fluidly at the other end. Dale stood with them, and felt a sickness in his throat. It was all wrong. Everything was going wrong. They were being railroaded.

The horn blared. It was the signal to conclude warm-ups, to move into position to start the game. The Little M's watched the Truckers cut off their drill and turn to carry their several new balls toward their bench. Mr. Bothner and Coach Burke were moving out, to receive and direct the players, Coach Burke gathering the balls and stuffing them into one of the school's green cloth bags.

The official was calling something to them. "Little M's, hey you, captain, over here," the man said again, and it was then, Dale would recall later, that he felt a sensation arise on the back of his neck. Something within him clicked. He was going to fight.

He walked over. He still did not know what he was going to do or say, but he knew that everything was different now. His team was being cheated, they were being railroaded. It was all he seemed to know.

Dale heard the official say to the Truckers, "Captain Dillard, step over here, please."

The man was going to have a word with the captains there before the scorer's table. It would be, Dale knew—as always in games in the double gym—an account of the gym and its lines, including mention of a cable which draped from the ceiling near center court and had never been hit by a ball in any case.

As the official concluded his remarks and looked to Joe and then to Dale, Dale said, "I'm lodging a protest. This is supposed to be a neutral site for play-offs and we're not being treated in that way, because we're not being allowed to warm up. It's not fair."

This stopped the official, at last, and had him looking at Dale. "How's that?" he said, with a small smile.

Dale pointed to the green ball bag behind the Truckers' bench, behind Coach Burke standing there. "Those balls they used belong to this school. I asked if we could use balls to warm up, and he said we had to bring our own. The other team didn't bring their own. That's not fair and it's your job to not let that happen."

"Now, Captain—what's your name again?"

"I didn't say my name. You didn't ask. You said to him 'Captain Dillard,' and you said to me 'hey you.' "

"Hey hey hey, hold on now. Let's not get carried away here."

"If you're not going to call the game fair and square, why call it at all?"

"Son, you had better take it easy, I'm warning you right now." The man's voice had changed and he was pointing a finger at Dale's chin.

Dale looked back at the man and at his finger. "Dale Wheeler," he said then. "My name's Dale Wheeler. I'm captain of the Little M's."

"Captain Wheeler," the official said. "Okay—Captain Wheeler? Now what is your complaint? You think the host school should have provided warm-up balls for your team, too, is that what you're saying?"

There again, the man's voice had changed, and others were watching now, Dale noticed. Mr. Bothner, Coach Burke, the scorekeeper, the timekeeper. "You got it," Dale said. "Balls and a warm-up. This is supposed to be a neutral site. That's what Coach Burke said himself. Only it isn't. We're being screwed already and the game hasn't even started yet."

"Whoa now, hey, let's just watch the language here, okay?" the official said.

Dale looked back and there was the sensation again, flickering like electricity from the back of his neck. "Language doesn't have anything to do with anything," he said. "That's not what this is about. If we're going to be cheated before the game even starts, and you're going to let them do it, then this game is being played under protest."

"Son, what is your name again? You had better calm down, I'm telling you."

"I'm calm. I already told you my name." Dale stood still, did not move—it was the only way he could think to hold his ground—even as he knew he was on the edge of losing control of himself, of perhaps breaking into tears, or going crazy and throwing over the official's table, swinging his fists at everybody.

"Captain Wheeler," the official said, more clearly, more softly. "Listen now. I didn't mean to offend you when I said 'Hey you,' if that's what I said. But you better do as I say concerning your language or you won't be playing in this game at all, because I'm prepared to put you out of this gym and out of this building, believe me."

"You on their side too? How many do they get on their side? You're saying it's okay for one team to cheat, and you tell the other team to watch its language."

The official only stared at him, wide-eyed in outrage but perhaps in astonishment, too. He glanced to the floor. Then, looking up, he said, calmly, as if to try a new tack, "Your protest is that you weren't allowed a warm-up? Your protest is the other team got to use school balls, and you didn't? Well, you want a warm-up, we'll give you a warm-up. It'll have to be quick, though. Coach—can you let these kids use a couple basketballs?"

Coach Burke, standing there to watch, leaned in another step and said, intently, "Host school is *not* obligated to furnish warm-up balls. It is in the rule book. I've said that about three times now."

"If this is a neutral site, how come he's telling everybody what to do?" Dale said.

"Hear that," Coach Burke said. "I told you this boy was a troublemaker."

"Just hold on there, Coach," the official said, turning

his anger, Dale could see, even more fiercely now in Coach
Burke's direction. "Let's get this problem solved, okay?"

"I'll say it again," Coach Burke said. "Host school is not
required to provide warm-up balls, or game balls either, for
playoffs, not in City League."

"You just did," Dale said.

"Irrespective," Coach Burke said.

This brought stares at Coach Burke from others standing
there, perhaps in disbelief—into which breach something
told Dale to go ahead and jump. "Thanks a lot, Coach
Burke," he said, turning away. "You should get a medal.
You're a credit to the human race. This game is being played
under protest."

Dale walked to his teammates, hearing at his back exclamations, a guffaw or two, even laughter, believing that
he had scored a bull's-eye.

In only a moment, Coach Burke was striding past them,
going, Dale knew, to the ball bin in the corner. Dale knew,
too, that only old rubber gym balls were kept in the bin,
as he watched Coach Burke unlatching and lifting the lid.
Dale said at once to his teammates, "*Don't touch these balls!
Don't even touch them! Screw these jerks! We'll play without
warming up! Don't touch them!*"

Hoots and shouts were coming from the stands by then,
and there was Coach Burke, one smoothly worn rubber ball
in hand and another at his feet as he closed the lid. Turning
toward the Little M's, he bowled one and the other ball in
their direction, and walked after them.

The Little M's stood in place. The balls came rolling
their way and they did not move, or stepped aside half a
step, looked down as the balls rolled by and watched them
roll across the floor to the Truckers' bench, where, as if the
balls were contagious, the Truckers standing there did not
touch them either, and they were fielded by a couple of junior
high boys sitting in the first row. Coach Burke walked by.

The two boys held the balls and looked around, not knowing what to do. A near-hush was passing over the crowd as it perceived that something unusual was taking place.

The chief official came out a few steps. "Captain Wheeler," he said. "Step over here, please."

Dale stepped over. So did Mr. Bothner and Coach Burke step closer. "Captain Wheeler, is your team declining the offer of warm-up?" the official said.

"If the host school is neutral," Dale said, "why do they provide new leather balls for one team, which are game balls, and those old worn-out balls for the other team? Is that neutral?"

The chief official suddenly laughed. "Coach Burke, I think Captain Wheeler may have you there," he said.

"I happen to know the rule book," Coach Burke said.

"I know the rule book too," Dale said. "I know every page of the rule book. It's twenty-seven pages long and it says there's supposed to be equal treatment at neutral play-off sites. That's what it says, but that's not what you're doing."

Faces turned to Coach Burke for his reply, but he offered nothing more than a scowl aimed at Dale.

"Nonetheless, Captain Wheeler, you have been offered balls for a warm-up," the official said. "You don't want to accept them, that's your business. The protest is lifted, I want that understood. Now do you want a warm-up, or not?"

Dale tried to think it out. "No," he said, turning away. "We'll beat them without a warm-up." He kept walking.

"Just go easy now, Captain Wheeler," the official said behind him. "Get your team ready. This game is going to start."

As Dale approached his teammates, someone bellowed from the stands, "WHEELER, WHAT'RE YOU DOING, YOU TRAITOR!"

Not looking, Dale flicked a middle finger toward the voice. Feeling betrayed in another wave by the remark, feeling misunderstood by his entire school, he tried to wall up his heart as he said to his teammates, "Game's going to start. No warm-up. I said we didn't need a warm-up. Let's beat these guys! Let's kill their ass!"

The horn blared again from the scorer's table.

Holding them a moment, Lucky said, "Let's do it to these jerks! COME ON!" Their huddle broke, their subs moved toward the bench, and they turned around to meet the Michigan Truckers, who, to their surprise, were, all of them, forming a line facing away, looking to the far end of the gym.

"Line up there for the national anthem," the second official said.

A little confused, as their subs had to return from the bench, the Little M's exchanged glances and grins as they also formed a line. Looking to the scoreboard, Dale realized there was a flag above it fixed to the wall. It was the first time he had ever had to stand for the national anthem before a game, and he hardly had time to think about it as a scratchy record began to emit music from speakers somewhere on high. In past years, he realized, the anthem had been played only downtown at the game for the entire city. "Ooh ooh say . . . can you see . . . ," a woman's voice was singing out.

Dale, arms at his sides, looked at the flag. The music ran through him and an old dream moved in his veins as, from there on high, the woman delivered the words. As she arrived at "O'er the la-and of the free, and the ho-oh-ome of the brave . . . ," Dale was ready again to either fight or cry.

•　•　•

Yet another delay occurred, however, for Coach Burke was up from the Truckers' bench, calling the chief official's attention to something, pointing to the clock under the flag. While almost everyone was looking at the clock, to see what the problem was, Dale kept looking at Coach Burke. The short man—he wore a sweater under his sport coat, over his white shirt and tie, even though the grip of winter had passed—had gotten to his feet from the Truckers' bench, between Mr. Bothner and the scorer's table. Anyone walking in would have thought he was the coach, or that the Truckers had two coaches.

The problem over—it had to do with resetting the clock—Coach Burke was sitting back down, and the chief official, game ball still in hand, having conferred with the timekeeper, was returning to the waiting players. All this time, looking at Coach Burke, Dale was wondering again why they were letting him run everything, and there again was the sensation playing upon his neck.

Walking to meet the official, Dale wasn't sure what he was going to say. "Our roster—we put in at the beginning of the year," he said. "We couldn't add any players, once the season started?"

"That's right," the official said.

"Can a team add coaches? How many coaches is a team allowed to have?"

"You know what?" the official said. "I think I've heard just about enough of you and enough of your complaints. We're going to play a basketball game here. That's what we're going to do, and it's going to be played fair, you can count on that."

Dale hesitated, started away, hesitated again, saying to himself, no, don't overdo it. Still, he knew he was right, knew the official was trying to railroad him, and it was as if he could not help what was going on inside him. Turning back yet again, he heard himself say, "I'm the captain—I have a right to speak for my team. It's not fair to say I can't speak for my team."

The official glared, stared as if he would like to throw Dale to the floor and kick him. Dale stared back. The man smiled, not in a friendly way. "You really think you're gonna steamroll me, don't you?" he said softly.

"No," Dale said.

"What's your problem—that's what I'd like to know."

Dale looked back at the man. "It's okay for Coach Burke to say something about the clock," he said. "Why isn't it okay for me to say something about how many coaches they have?"

"You sound like a broken record, you know that."

"I have a right—as captain—to ask a question. That's all I did, was ask a question."

"What is your question?"

"Why is Coach Burke on their bench? Is his name on their roster? I know the rule book. Is his name on their roster or not?"

The man continued studying him. Dale stared back in turn, and it was the man who glanced to the side. "Okay," he said. "Okay. I'll check this out. But don't try my patience anymore. I happen to know the rule book too, okay? If he's listed as an assistant coach, he's allowed to be on the bench."

Dale stood there as the official turned and carried the game ball with him once more to the scorer's table. Leaning in, he spoke to the timekeeper, who, turning an ear to listen, reached to a leather bag on the floor, near his feet, from which he removed a sheaf of papers. Angling the papers for both to read at once, he flipped over, settled on a page, and ran his finger down. Straightening up, pausing, the official stepped over to Coach Burke and Mr. Bothner, where both sat watching as if to ask what in the world is going on now. The two stood up to talk.

As the official spoke to them, and Dale watched, a small

bomb seemed to go off in their midst as Coach Burke's hands flew up all at once and he swung his head around. He seemed to jump once on his feet, to stamp like Adolf Hitler. He motioned to the table, to the floor, and generally to Dale, and continued talking wildly in harsh whispers. The three men moved to the table, as the timekeeper once more turned the sheaf of papers to be read. Dale was surprised at the emotion coming into his heart. He turned his back on the scene, turned as sharply as a bullfighter defying a maddened animal. Orange and black, take no flak.

Nearby, startling Dale even as he spoke softly, Sonny Joe Dillard said, "What is this crap, Wheeler, what're you doing now?"

Dale looked at Sonny Joe. "Blow it out your ass, you stupid jerk!" he said, and his own ears and neck prickled again with anger, emotion, a desire to fight. No one talked like that to Joe Dillard.

A sudden noise had them looking to the bench and scorer's table. At center was Coach Burke, his face as red as Dale had ever seen a man's face. He was leaving the bench, making his way up into the bleachers, stepping up angrily between spectators, where, turning and squeezing into a space, he sat down, turned around, and glared with a look meant to assassinate. Scattered applause and laughter traveled over the crowd. Dale turned back yet again to center court.

The chief official returned. "Coach Burke," the man said, all around, "was not on the Michigan Truckers' roster as a coach and therefore cannot sit on their bench. All of you, listen to me now," he added, waving a hand.

They closed some around him. "I'm gonna tell you something," he said. "This game is going to be fairly played and it's going to be fairly officiated. Some of you seem to think everybody's out to take advantage of you. Well, I want you to know, as long as I'm calling this game, it's going to be called fairly. I don't know whatever happened around here in the past, and I don't want to know. What we're gonna do is play a basketball game, and that's where I'd advise all of you to put your energies. Okay? I'm talking to you, Captain Wheeler, if you are interested in finishing this game. I hope you understand me, because I have had it with this display!"

Dale thought to speak, but did not. He simply held the man's gaze.

"Now line it up," the man said. "I am not saying any more. Line it up! This game is going to be decided on the floor. Line it up! NOW!"

Dale moved back with his teammates, then the five starters reapproached the center. The three front-line players on each side shouldered in, crouched in preparation for the jump. Dale remained a few steps outside the circle. The official was about to loft the ball. There were the two Bothner brothers, easy to spot among his former teammates, both bigger and heavier, more muscular than he had imagined. The older brother, Keith, was on the line adjacent to Grady Devlin; the younger boy, Karl, was behind the circle in a position similar to Dale's, although back two or three, even four added steps, altogether defensive, leaving an inviting space between himself and the location of the jump.

"Boys, let's have a good clean game now," the official said. "Good luck."

The younger Bothner boy was stepping back still another step, Dale noticed, as the official had the ball ready to loft. Dale had already been considering an attempted steal, and in this instant he decided yes, why not. Yes, he thought. Yes. He had seen it done at the park. Sonny Joe would win the jump, Dale calculated—he had never seen Sonny Joe not win a jump. Joe would tip the ball directly back to Karl Bothner, as Joe had so many times tipped it to him. Yes, Dale thought, and he sneaked another half step to the side. A sudden dash-spurt, he calculated, and even if he missed the steal, it would be a Comanche storm upon Karl Bothner, maybe to force a bad pass, or to tie him up. At least he would throw a scare into him.

Dale slid over one more step, and part of another as everyone, crouched, tensed, was looking for the appearance of the ball in the air between the centers. Anticipating the toss, seeing the official's arm start up, Dale broke, exploded like a sprinter, slapped the ball in the air, slapped it ahead and to the left and continued after it, dribbled it on first contact on the run as he shot past the startled Karl Bothner and, determined not to miss, as he took it to the basket from the right side, knowing Karl Bothner might be reaching to slap at him, went into a turn—a shot from the park—and put it away off the board, spinning away and coming down to see it break the threads, continuing immediately to defense as a gasp and applause came from the crowd.

It worked! It was the most satisfying, perhaps the most successful shot he had ever made. It worked! No shot in the park, or in any other game, had ever been better, and his teammates knew it, too, as they called and cheered in their circling around to defense. "Way to go, Dale!" "Great shot!" "Jesus, way to go!" "That's the way!" "Little Wheel, that's the way! We can win this game!"

Dale took in the words, took in, too, the scattered ongoing response from the crowd. *Play as in the park!* he was saying to himself. *Play as in the park! Hang loose and take charge! Be cool and take charge! Do it!* He had his eyes on defense, as he was sidestepping, backstepping, watching as the Truckers put the ball in play. Two to nothing, he thought. The Little M's were ahead of the dirty, cheating sonofabitches, two to nothing.

The Truckers' forwards had loped by, and here were the guards bringing along the ball. But for the Bothners, they were his old teammates and this was it. It's probably the first time all year they've been behind, he thought. Has to be. He avoided eye contact; he eyed the ball, eyed the giveaway chest-bone area, kept his hands out, fingers outspread, sidestepped, backstepped with the movement of the ball. *Beat these jerks!* he said to himself. *Beat 'em!*

Karl Bothner. Number 9. Dale kept his eyes on the top of the 9 on the front of the boy's shirt, kept the ball in sight, too, kept his hands out, sidestepped. The boy raised a single finger, to signal his teammates as he dribbled to the side. Set plays. Dale was impressed, and threatened, too, all at once, for neither the Little M's nor any other team he had played on had used or been taught set plays.

The ball was passed to Hal Doyle, as he came out from his corner, and as a rotation was started, Karl Bothner moved to Hal Doyle's position, received the ball there in turn. Dale collapsed back toward the center only to see, over his shoulder to the other side, a sharp pass move the ball back to Hal Doyle and back in at once to Sonny Joe, who—as both Chub and Lucky were screened, as if magically—pivoted without dribbling and laid it in off the board.

The score was tied.

"TIME!" Dale called. "Time out!"

A whistle blew.

"What happened?" Dale said as the Little M's gathered near the end line. "He was all alone!"

"We got blocked out!" Chub said at the same time that Lucky and Grady each said, "I got blocked out!"

"We gotta double-team Joe Dillard!" Dale said. "We got to! They'll eat us alive! Triple-team him! All three of you! Make somebody else shoot! Somebody blocks you, knock him down, take a foul if you have too! Jesus! Sonny Joe will just kill us! Triple-team him! All three of you! Let's go!"

Breaking huddle, they loped to their positions as the official tweeted his whistle and handed over the ball. Dale inbounded to Emmett, took the ball back in a return pass, moved it downcourt.

"HEY, GOOD TIME OUT, WHEELER!" someone shouted.

"TRAITOR!" someone else called.

"GOOD TIME OUT!" the first voice called back.

Dale moved the ball over the center line. He reminded himself to stop listening, to close his hearing to anything anyone might call from the stands. He passed off to Emmett, took a pass back. Moving, dribbling to the right, for the hell of it he raised two fingers of his left hand, drew guffaws at once from Lucky and Grady, and at once he passed to Lucky in the corner and followed the pass, as Lucky passed inside to Chub.

Going up to shoot from five to six feet, Chub found the hands and arms of Sonny Joe and Hal Doyle all over him, and even as he got his shot off, he missed everything and the ball was taken from the air on the left side by bulky Keith Bothner, who passed immediately upcourt to one of his teammates. Dale and the rest of the Little M's raced back downcourt on defense.

There, in a moment, was Karl Bothner moving the ball to the side, looking things over, looking to initiate a play. Jealousy stabbed at Dale, as he moved with him, hurt that he did not know these plays, had not learned these certain skills, that he had been denied this, cheated, as a real basketball player, out of this, too.

Two fingers were raised this time! Jerk! Dale thought. At the same time, Karl Bothner passed off and moved, as another play was being executed. Two passes followed quickly. Under the basket, however, Chub, Grady, and Lucky pushed, swarmed, jumped, and held their own around Sonny Joe, forcing him to pass the ball out to Keith Bothner, who shot from some twelve feet, overshot the basket entirely, and as Lucky pulled the ball out of the air, Dale was already running.

Shadowed by Karl Bothner, not receiving a pass, Dale circled back, took a pass there from Grady, passed to Lucky in the corner, took the ball back in another pass from Lucky, passed it back at once to Lucky, watched him go up, shoot, and score. Moving past him, going downcourt, Lucky made a fist to Dale, said, "Good pass!" as Dale said after him, in turn, "Keep shooting! Keep going in like that!"

The game went along, settled into a rhythm. The teams traded baskets, traded misses, turnovers, steals, fouls, traded more baskets, free throws, more misses. The players perspired, gasped for air, kept moving. They seemed to be evenly matched, with an edge going to the Little M's for their aggressiveness and tenacity. It was another real game, a playoff game which was taking the players, and most of the spectators, too—maybe the spectators and coaches more than the players—on an extended, heart-squeezing roller-coaster ride.

The Little M's stayed ahead, but only by two or three or four points. Once they went up by five, and it ran through Dale's mind that if they could get to seven, just seven, they could have something of a cushion, and with something of a cushion they could absorb a run of points against them, could actually think—no, he would not say it to himself, wouldn't let himself even think it. At once then, on an intercepted pass from Emmett, their lead was cut back to three, and Dale blamed himself for even daring to think as he had at a time like that. Don't do that! he told himself. Don't even think like that! Be smart all the way!

Frustration and instances of satisfaction accompanied them all as they moved back and forth, end to end, raced, grabbed, jumped, tried to pull in needed air. Chub, Grady, and Lucky circled, pressed, collapsed as physically as possible upon Sonny Joe, before and after he received the ball, drawing swung elbows and facial expressions from Joe, too, and exclamations to one referee or another as he looked for fouls to be called, and faint smirks when calls went his way. The triple-teaming was working. Joe was forced to pass back out, or forced to send up one of his long looping hook shots, which, two or three times out of four, found iron or board alone and failed to find the precious twine skirt waiting to whip its magical tail and set off a response from the crowd.

As Sonny Joe shot less, Keith Bothner shot more, but scored so rarely that Grady began to leave the bulky boy all but free to get off his wooden, knee-raised release. However tall, and however long his arms, he was awkward in his bulkiness, often shot too hard, without a touch, or with too small an arc, or simply missed the target by a foot or two. Or his shots would *clunk!* the rim and ricochet sharply into someone below. Missing, he frowned, as if apologetically; the couple times he did score, closer in, he seemed unable to keep himself from grinning, from showing a giddiness and stealing glances to the bench.

At the other end, the Truckers were also tightening up their defense. Shots and moves by Chub, Grady, or Lucky anywhere close to the basket were becoming increasingly difficult. Using a zone, and working in substitutions where the Little M's worked in none, the Truckers kept intensifying their defense and, after time-outs and huddles with Mr. Bothner, introducing new strategies. At last, as the difficulty of moving the ball inside continued, Dale began to consider shooting from outside. If he could score only once or twice, he thought, their lead might increase, might become a real lead, and the Truckers would be forced to loosen up some on the inside.

No opportunity presented itself before Chub, on a sudden sharp pass from Lucky, moved under Sonny Joe and got off a shot which went directly into the basket. Their lead was back to four.

End to end, scores, misses, rebounds, passes. Fouls and whistles. Hands on hips, circling to pull in air before toeing to the line for free throws.

Now their lead was three points. Dale knew the score without looking to the scoreboard, and he looked to see not the score but the time remaining. With less than two minutes in the half, he had an opening from thirteen or fourteen feet on a pass back out from Lucky. Almost automatically, even as he had been waiting for the chance, he went up, aimed, looked, pulled the trigger.

Whipp!

The thrill sensation shot through him. The sensation ran from heart to groin to heart as the crowd roared. He turned to defense with a vengeance. And, hardly thirty seconds later—in a similar situation, as if the Truckers were unafraid of the shot—he went up as before, found the rim, locked, fired.

Whipp!

If the response from the crowd was ragged on the first shot, this time it was sharp and clear, as the same wild thrill shot through Dale. A seven-point lead. Lucky, going past him, had fire in his eyes. *"We can beat these guys! Let's do it!"*

To his own amazement, Dale scored still another shot from outside hardly a moment later. He was looking to whip the ball inside, and it was a shot he knew he should not take, but then the ball banged off board and rim and found its way through the precious skirt waiting below. However lucky the shot, a great roar-hoot came from the crowd. The Little M's were ahead by nine points.

The Truckers called time.

The Little M's also huddled, and Dale, crouching in the center, had a new idea, which he spat out frantically in the midst of all their gasping for air and flinging, arm-wiping of sweat. *"Full-court press!"* he said. *"Hold back and then*

*jump on them! Full-court press! The rest of the half! Let's
do it!"*

In a moment, as the Truckers came back to inbound the
ball, the Little M's exploded upon them all at once from
mid-court. The Truckers' forwards came running back, and
even as a wide bounce pass got the ball to Keith Bothner—
brother to brother—the Little M's swarmed the tall, bulky
boy at once, and Grady came up with the ball, passed at
once to Lucky, who passed to Chub as he was going to the
basket, and Chub laid it in over the rim down the center.
As the Truckers moved to inbound the ball, the horn blared.

The first half was over. The Little M's were up by eleven
points. A miracle of some kind seemed to be in the making.

Everyone on the floor was turning to look at the clock
on the far wall. Dale looked, too, although he was certain
he knew the numbers. He looked to see them in any case,
to take in the thrill, to let it give his heart a charge. There
were the lines of white bulbs: HOME 28/VISITORS 39. The
sensation squeezed his heart, and he glimpsed something
like eternity.

Gathering at their bench, the Little M's hesitated before
moving toward the tunnel. It was as if they did not want to
leave the amazing situation in which they found themselves.
Up by eleven. The crowd was quiet, in shock, it seemed,
as they walked across the floor. The ragged visitors up by
eleven! Over the polished machine which was their own
Michigan Truckers! It cannot be, the silence seemed to say.
It cannot be. Something is wrong.

Dale avoided eye contact with his teammates. They all
seemed to be doing the same, as if to not pop the balloon,
certainly not to celebrate ahead of time. Work to be done,
their expressions seemed to say. It sure isn't over yet. (But
an eleven-point lead! Who would have ever believed they'd
go in at halftime with an eleven-point lead?!)

At their backs all at once, as they were reaching the

tunnel, there came an amount of shouting, and looking back, Dale saw that the Truckers were being called and herded the other way. There was Coach Burke, in the middle of things again, standing with a key attached to a line at his waist, unlocking the door to the girls' locker room. There, too, was Mr. Bothner, angrily waving the Truckers back in that direction. An emergency, Dale thought. They're going to use the girls' locker room. They're down by eleven. It's an emergency. God—can it be true?

Entering the locker room, and their aisle, the Little M's still avoided eye contact, even as a yelp came out here and there. Lucky cut loose with a long howl, like a dog, and at once they were all pushing around and laughing like first graders. "WE CAN BEAT THESE JERKS!" Lucky bellowed. "WE CAN! WE CAN DO IT! *WE CAN DO IT!!*"

Dale sat on the bench. They were up by eleven at the half. Over the Michigan Truckers. Was this happiness? Oh, this was it. This was everything. This. Yes, this. Bang, bang, bang! He'd scored three times in a row from outside. He had. He really had. Bang, bang, bang! Commandos strike at dawn! The deed was being done!

He sat with the slightest grin on his face, and in silence. Thirty-nine points. It was a lot of points, even for the last year of City League. No, don't count your points, he told himself. And he did not, even as he had to struggle against his mind running up his stats all on its own. Don't be a fool—play it cool!

His teammates. They played and shot well, he realized. They're good athletes, he realized. Maybe their team wasn't real well organized, nor were their fathers all over the place telling everybody what to do, but they were good athletes. Athletes who had done it themselves—who were ahead! He sat there in silence still, and if his mind was not entirely aware, his heart knew clearly that these now were his friends, he liked all things about them, and knew, alas, that he was prepared to die for them, that he was ready to die for his team and for this game, that it was all things to him now.

"Dale, man, you are having the game of your life!" Grady said.

"So are you," Dale said. "Everybody is."

"I mean it," Grady said. "Just keep it up. We'll beat these jerks. We'll go downtown on Saturday and do the City!"

"I can taste it," Chub said. "Goddam—I can taste it!"

"So can I," Lucky said. "Let's just play the same game second half. Play tough. Don't get cautious. We're gonna beat these guys!"

Only later would Dale realize that no cigarettes were brought out during this halftime, for the first time all year. The game had them in its grip.

"Let's not panic," Chub said. "Let's stay cool and keep pressing, but don't panic."

"Let's kick ass!" Lucky said.

"Let's do it!" Dale said. "Let's really do it!"

Legs heavier, hearts in no way jitter free, the Little M's passed back through the tunnel to reenter the vast, noisy space. Shouts, screams, boos flew through the air. A number of the calls, Dale half-perceived—against his instructions to himself—included his name.

The Truckers had yet to appear. They were late returning to the floor. Dale imagined them being harangued madly by Coach Burke until he was out of breath and red as a tomato again, and by Mr. Bothner, too, given the smoke which seemed to be coming from the giant man's ears as he had waved them into the girls' locker room. A thought ran through Dale's mind, to ask for a technical for delay of game, but he decided to forget it, to leave well enough alone.

Dale was experiencing superstitious notions. Should they warm up this time? Should they not? Should they do exactly as they had for the first half? "Maybe we shouldn't warm up this time either," he said to his teammates, as they had crossed the floor to their bench.

"Let's shoot around," Chub said. "Let's loosen up."

"I don't know—you think we should?" Dale said.

"What do you mean?" Grady said.

"I don't know—I don't want to break the spell," Dale said.

"Ah, let's warm up," Grady said.

As captain, Dale went to the scorer's table, where the officials were standing, waiting to start the second half. "Can we use a couple balls this time?" Dale said.

The chief referee held up both hands in mock surrender. "Anything you say, Captain. Anything you say. Sure don't wanna go to court again this time." The man was smiling, however, and the men around him laughed.

Dale, not knowing what to say, only smiled in turn. He walked back to his teammates with two of the pebbly, new leather balls, wondering yet again if it was a mistake to change anything this half, to surrender their anger in any way. Or their pride. That's what it was, he thought, as he joined in shooting around. They had taken his pride from him. When the Michigan Truckers left him off their team, it had leveled his pride. Now, ahead by eleven, his pride was coming back. No, don't even think about it, he cautioned himself. Not now. Not yet. Just let it be there, he told himself as he went to the board to take down a rebound. Stop thinking!

He heard then—they all did—a voice bellow from the stands, "BEST PLAYER ON YOUR TEAM IS FROM OUR SCHOOL, YOU HILLBILLIES!" This drew a grin from Lucky, and from Dale, too, while they otherwise acted as if they had not heard the voice.

The Truckers came out. Dale looked, and knew at once that something was different. Burkebutt and Mr. Bothner must have taken them apart, he thought, because he had never seen players look so serious or so stricken after a dressing-down. Dale wondered if it would work. Would they be able to respond?

They were not going to warm up. The Truckers, Dale realized, were not going to warm up! They moved to their bench, where the subs took their seats. The starting five went directly to center court. They were ready to play. Dale felt as if something else had been taken from him, from his team.

The horn blared, the official tweeted his whistle, and the Little M's also moved to center court to take their positions. The Truckers, Dale noticed, were glaring, but mostly at the floor, avoiding eye contact.

They lined up. Crouched. Dale decided not to try for an interception this time, and on the jump, at once, something went wrong for the Little M's. Sonny Joe controlled the ball, tipped it on an angle directly to Karl Bothner and, as the Little M's backpedaled downcourt into their zone, Joe took a return pass between them near the freethrow line, turned, went up to shoot, and scored, from about twelve feet. He's good, Dale said to himself. The bastard is so good. He could see their strategy, too, to move Joe out, to have him shoot from around the circle, and when they came out after him, he would pass inside to one of their forwards going to the basket. Even Keith Bothner, Dale thought, could lay it in off the board.

Dale did not call a time-out. Not yet, he thought. He wasn't sure what was happening, only that the Truckers' offense was different. But so was their defense different, as Karl Bothner was bird-dogging their movement downcourt, darting back and forth to slow it down as much as he could. Not a press, as he had thought they might try, just this irritating pressure from one player. What also ran through Dale's mind, as he took a return pass from Emmett and Karl Bothner came running at him—he passed off to Lucky—was that his own team, coachless, had no strategies, nor any wrinkles or irritants to try unless they used a time-out to concoct something on the spot.

Lucky returned the ball to him, and Dale moved it back out and around, looking to Emmett but also to Chub and Grady as they moved in anticipation. The Truckers' defense, at least for now, was intense, ferocious. It was, of course, how the Little M's had opened the game, and this thought, too, was worrisome to Dale. The underdog's rage seemed to have gone over to the other side. He passed off again. There was no penetrating the frenzied Truckers' zone. Don't think like a loser, Dale told himself. Think positive. Be a leader. Take charge. Don't let the Truckers take over the game.

So it was that Dale considered shooting again from out-side. It would be a risk. The idea seemed sound, that a score might take away the edge the Truckers had brought from the locker room. It might scare them, put them back on the defensive. At the same time, there was a thought somewhere in his mind that he should not gamble in any way, that he, they, should take no chances. It wasn't the moment to gamble, was it? He took the ball on a return pass from Lucky. He dribbled, moved back to Lucky's side. The thought returned to his mind to go for it. Give them a sharp punch in the nose. It could put the Truckers over the edge, make them panic. It could ice the game. Be a leader!

The ball came back again from Lucky. Dale went up. Karl Bothner was all over him as he got off his shot. He missed. The ball hit the rim, was ripped from the air by Sonny Joe with his speed and reach, was passed off, and Dale knew at once that the consequences were worse than he had imagined. He was too far out. Emmett had been caught off guard. The Truckers went in and Hal Doyle scored going under the basket. The punch was not given but received, and it stung.

The crowd reacted. A turnaround was what they wanted, and anticipation was in the air. In little more than a minute, four points had been recovered.

"Jesuschrist, pass it in!" Chub said to Dale, circling back past him on his way downcourt.

A moment later, when another shot missed—this time by Lucky—and the Truckers took down the rebound yet again and went on to score, Sonny Joe popping in another jumper from ten feet, Dale called time. Their eleven-point lead had been cut to five.

They huddled. "You're gonna have to stay out with Joe," Dale said to Chub. "We can't let him take that outside shot; he'll kill us out there."

"Well, don't you take those long shots!" Chub said. "Stop trying to be a goddam hero!"

Dale's heart sank. "Hey, cool it," Lucky said. "Let's play the game."

"It was a dumb shot," Dale said.

As they moved to inbound the ball, the Truckers had another surprise. There they were, all at once, in a sudden, swarming full-court press. Within the surprise was another surprise; the press was not led by their guards but by their three biggest players, Joe Dillard, Keith Bothner, and Hal Doyle. All at once, with their enormous arms, they were all over Dale as he scrambled to try to inbound the ball along the end line. Hands, legs, feet, arms chopped wildly before him. At last, on a fake, seeing Lucky moving on the run, he got off a bounce pass under Keith Bothner's arm. At once, though, the two swarmed Lucky, and as Lucky returned the ball to Dale, Keith Bothner got some fingers on it, dove after it, as did Dale, toward the center circle, and the two ended up in a frantic grapple on the floor as the whistle blew.

"Jump ball!" the official said.

As they got to their feet, the second official was carrying the ball to the foul circle before the basket of the Little M's, even as Dale was certain the tie-up had been much closer to the center circle. "What're you doing?" he cried. "That has to be jumped in the center!"

"Jump ball here!" the man said.

"Hey, come on!" Dale said. "What is this?"

"Tie-up was closest to this circle, let's go!" the man said.

"The hell it was!" Dale said.

"You watch that tongue or I'm putting you out of this game!" the man said.

Dale moved to the other official. "What is this?" he said. "You said this was going to be a fair game! Jump goes to the nearest circle!"

"He called it, that's how he saw it," the chief official said. "Line it up or I'm calling a technical!"

"Can I have an explanation?" Dale said. "I'm the captain, I'm requesting an explanation."

The chief official held a palm toward Dale, to tell him to shut up, but he did turn to the second official to lean in and confer. Quickly he turned back. "Jump ball right there where he said," he said. "It's his call."

The Little M's moved along. "Why didn't he blow his whistle closer to that circle?" Dale said.

"You better play ball and shut up, number five, or I'm calling a technical on you," the chief official said.

"Can I ask one question?" Dale said. "One question. I'm the captain."

"One question," the chief official said. "That's it."

"I just questioned that call," Dale said, aware of a frantic gasp in his voice. "That's all I did. And he said he was going to put me out of the game. I'm the captain. I have the right to question a call. He can call a technical. But he can't just put me out of the game. Because he doesn't like me. The call was wrong and you know it—and you said we were going to have a fair game. That's what you said."

The man was looking at him, less in anger this time than in something like concern. "Son," he said. "I think you better get a hold of yourself. This isn't a court of law, this is a basketball game."

"I can question a call," Dale said.

"You disputed the call. He doesn't have to put up with that, and neither do I. You better just play the game, believe me, because I am about to put you out of this game myself. For your own good. Jump ball!"

"So he can call a technical!" Dale said. "You threaten to put people out of a game, it takes the fight out of their team! That's not fair, and you said—"

"*Jump ball!*" the man said.

Dale was looking down, between his knees, taking in breaths. He looked back up, stepped over toward the circle before the basket the Little M's were defending. "You know he says that because we don't have a bunch of coaches over there," Dale said.

Before the official had a chance to reply, there was Grady at Dale's side, his sweaty arm coming around his neck. "Come on, Dale, forget it," he said, close by. "Let's play the game."

Dale moved with him, looking down, still taking in air. On a glance, as he stepped over to the line, he saw that other players were watching him, taking looks at him, as if it were true that he was losing it.

He shouldered in, crouched, beside bulky Keith Bothner. Just then, from the stands, someone bellowed, "STUPID REF—JUMP BALL SHOULD BE IN THE MIDDLE—WHAT THE HELL YOU DOING?!"

There was anger in the shout. It sent a charge into Dale.

He turned from his crouch, took a breath. He returned to the crouch. There was the ball in the official's hand near his shoulder, being prepared for its loft between them. Dale sensed, more than saw, the bulk of Keith Bothner crouched beside him, also tensing for the jump, six or seven inches taller, his arms and hands so much longer and heavier. As the ball went up, as if in slow motion, Dale was already leaving his feet on an angle.

His shoulder massed into the shoulder bones and slippery sweat of the other boy, nudging, tipping, knocking him off balance and out of the way before he even got himself launched, leaving the ball hanging uncontested in the air— while Keith Bothner was stumbling to regain his balance— and Dale tapped it directly back to Emmett. Play continued. No whistle blew. Keith Bothner was coming back, looking around wild-eyed, and as Dale received the ball back from Emmett and started moving it downcourt, looking for his teammates, a sudden loud whistle blew and stopped them all.

The commotion was on the side of the court, before the scorer's table. Mr. Bothner was on the floor, on the playing surface, red-faced, pointing at Dale, roaring, "THAT IS A DIRTY PLAYER! YOU! YES, YOU, NUMBER FIVE! YOU ARE A DIRTY PLAYER, THAT'S WHAT YOU ARE! GET THAT KID OUT OF THIS GAME! HE IS A DIRTY PLAYER! GET HIM OUT OF THIS GAME!!"

Both officials, as if to contain Mr. Bothner, were closing around him with arms and hands out. Making contact, they turned him, guided him toward his own bench, even as he continued looking over them at Dale, out on the floor. Taking a moment to settle him down, the chief official returned toward center court, indicating with his fingers that he wanted the ball. "Bench technical," he said over his shoulder to the scorer's table. "Michigan Truckers—bench technical."

Dale felt little at being called a dirty player, unless it was satisfaction. He had gotten the man's attention. The man who had removed him from his own team, who had taken away his dream. And he wasn't a dirty player, he said to himself. He was only playing to win. It was all he was doing. He wasn't here to lose; he was here to win.

His teammates were around him, smiling over the outbreak, gasping for air. "You shoot it," Lucky said. "You're the dirty player, you shoot it."

Following the official, who carried the ball, Dale walked to the free-throw line. Shouts and hoots came from the stands. As Dale readied himself, the man handed him the ball. "One shot," he said.

Dale positioned his toes near the line, bounced the ball. He looked to the rim, bounced the ball again. The shouts from the stands increased. Do it now, Dale told himself. Don't think about it. He shot. Missed. His heart sank. The ball hit the rear of the rim, hit a dead spot, bounced to the front of the rim, fell off the side to the floor. Applause and hoots came from all around as Dale turned back to rejoin his team. Don't think, he told himself again, knowing he had invested more in the free shot than he wanted to admit. Don't think, he told himself.

Play continued and so did the Truckers' manic full-court press. The Little M's moved the ball downcourt, passed and passed and passed, tried to work the ball inside for good shots, to no avail, passed some more, until someone—it seemed everyone gave in to the temptation—tried what seemed a possible shot only to have two or three Truckers suddenly all over him, and all over the board to take down the rebound when the shot was missed.

They moved back on defense, tried in turn to be as tenacious as the Truckers. There was Mr. Bothner, Dale noticed, pacing the sideline before his bench, waving his hands, shouting instructions, more into the game than any City League or Scholastic League coach he had ever seen. In one glimpse, Dale saw the enormous man turn and in near-violence fire something—it looked like a wad of paper—at his own bench.

The Truckers kept coming back, kept cutting the lead. Free throws were made and missed, shots made and missed. Dale lost track of the score for a time and purposely did not look to the scoreboard to check it out. Maybe their lead was four points, maybe five or six. Three. He didn't want to know. Try harder, he told himself. Harder! He wanted to see four straight Little M's points racked up, or five or six, then he'd look up and read the score.

In another moment, inbounding the ball at mid-court but still against the crazed, wild-handed press, Sonny Joe deflected the ball, and Dale, running after it, ended up in another wild floor grapple, this time with Karl Bothner. The whistle blew. "Jump ball, jump ball!" the official said.

Dale did not release the ball. He had relaxed some, but kept his hands on the ball, and suddenly he ripped it out of the younger boy's hands. Angered and wild at once, the boy came right back, not at Dale as much as at the ball, as if the contest at hand was to recover the ball, no matter what. The whistle blew again, more sharply, and the official snapped, "That's it! Enough! Jump ball!" as both officials moved in to separate them.

Karl Bothner had a nail grip on Dale's wrist by then, and when Dale whipped his hands back, violently this time, letting the ball fly away, his right fist came up doubled and he was ready to swing at the boy—who was similarly pos-sessed—ready to try to punch him out, to tear him apart. Dale had hardly made a step, however, before he was grabbed by the chief official, who hissed into his ear as he swung him around, *"Enough, right now, or you are out of this game!"*

Dale, in the bear hug from behind, could not have continued if he had tried, but again his attention and the attention of all, the man's son included, was turned to the side. There was Mr. Bothner, being restrained near the scorer's table by the scorekeeper and by little Coach Burke. The giant man was pointing, sputtering, bellowing over them, "THROW THAT NUMBER FIVE OUT OF THIS GAME! GET HIM OUT OF HERE! HE HAS NO BUSINESS IN THIS GAME! GET HIM OUT OF HERE!! HE IS A DIRTY PLAYER!! GET HIM OUT OF HERE!!"

The official holding Dale had released him, to go help the others control Mr. Bothner. Dale stood gasping. The players from both teams, standing, gasping, and most of the spectators, even as they were standing, simply watched the spectacle. Mr. Bothner, as one of his hands whipped up several times to accentuate whatever it was he was saying, was guided back to his bench. Once there, he was persuaded to sit down, and the chief official, coming back onto the court, motioned a finger to Dale, to indicate that he wanted to say something to him. To the other players, in general, he said, "Jump ball, right there, in one second."

To Dale, close by, the man said, "In about a minute. You. And their coach. Are leaving this floor. And this gym. Do you hear me? I have never seen such a display. *Do you hear what I'm saying?*"

Dale, head down, was still breathing hard, and nodding almost automatically. Still, he got his eyes to rise, his eyes alone, to meet the man's eyes. "He was," Dale managed to say. "On the floor. Two. Two technicals. You're out. That's in the book."

The man's eyes closed. His head turned down, and his eyes remained closed for several seconds, time needed, it seemed, to restrain himself from attempting to throttle the person before him. Looking up, he said, almost calmly, "I don't believe you. What are you. A shithouse lawyer? Or a basketball player? I am not putting that man out of this game. I am not going to do it."

"It's in the book," Dale said. "Automatic technical. Two technicals. Coach has to leave the floor. It was just a jump ball. Loose ball. Are they allowed to have six players—?"

"Just shut up. Right now. Just shut up. One more word, goddammit. One more word and you are gone. One more. I mean it. Unsportsmanlike conduct. I have to, I'll carry you out of here. I'll throw you in the goddam street. Jump ball." He was turning back. "Jump ball! Right now! Line it up! JUMP BALL!"

Dale hesitated still. He thought to say the game was being played under protest, but did not. He believed now that he would be bounced if he spoke, and he did not want to be bounced. He walked to center court. After all, weren't they still ahead?

Moving to the line, against his better judgment, he glanced to the scoreboard. He was surprised by the time remaining. The clock showed 3:07. Where had the time gone? The score also surprised him. HOME 49/VISITORS 50. They were ahead by one point.

Less than two minutes remained when the Little M's made their last run of the game. Scoring two straight baskets, they returned their lead to five. Dale had to check the scoreboard again to be certain of the numbers. Yes, their lead was five points. He also took in from the clock that 1:10 remained, and he wondered if time was on their side. At once, it seemed, the Truckers scored again—Hal Doyle went in untouched—cutting the lead to three.

There again, all over them, was the maddening full-court press.

Using Sonny Joe at the center of the storm, Dale knew, was a brilliant move. It defied the usual, was something Coach Burke had never tried. Joe, with his reach and speed, his brains and confidence, his energy and even his faintly malicious smile, centered the most formidable storming defense any of them had ever had to face. All along there had been more forced turnovers, tie-ups, passes tipped, slapped, kicked away, intercepted than any of them had ever seen.

The Truckers scored again, returning the lead to one. Dale tried to call a time-out, but Grady said he thought they'd used them all. Panic was gripping them, it was clear. If they gave up a technical, it could be the tying point. Dale moved to inbound the ball, was swarmed over by Keith Bothner and Sonny Joe yet again. He moved along the end line, faked, faked again, got off a pass toward Grady, and, a shock to him, Sonny Joe simply snatched the ball out of the air, dribbled back one step, and laid it in. The gym exploded with applause. For the first time in the entire game the Truckers were ahead.

It was Dale's only clear turnover of the game—he was outraged with himself over committing such an error— and even as his teammates all had marks and bad moves against them, in his mind it was the worst mistake of the game, of the year, of his life. "Time out!" he called. "Time out!"

"No, no," Grady was saying, running to try and get him to inbound the ball again.

"Technical, no time-outs remaining!" the chief official said, motioning to have the ball turned over to him. "Technical, number five, no time-outs remaining."

They had to stand back as Sonny Joe shot the ball. Dale stood watching, feeling numb.

Whipp!

They were down by two. Again, the crowd exploded. Joe,

returning to mid-court, wore his faint smile. The Truckers retained possession and would inbound the ball.

The nightmarish dismantling of the Little M's continued through the remaining seconds. Panic had them by the throat, no one more, it seemed to Dale, then himself. He stood by to watch Sonny Joe shoot in two more free throws, and when he glanced to the clock and saw 00:13, he knew it was over.

Another technical was called, on Lucky, for profanity, although Dale did not hear what he had said. Nor did he look at the clock again.

This time Mr. Bothner chose his youngest son to shoot the free throw. The Truckers' bench players were all on their feet by now, jumping around, calling out, celebrating their victory snatched from the jaws of defeat. Dale stood at mid-court, glanced toward the Truckers' bench, looked to the floor. Mr. Bothner was smiling and jubilant now.

Karl Bothner made the free throw. Dale watched the boy shoot and he wondered what it was at the beginning of the season that had him imagining being praised by the man over his own sons. That was so dumb. What a fool he had been. It was the only moment in the game when he felt his eyes film over, close to a childish breakdown.

The Truckers retained possession. Karl Bothner inbounded the ball, a gleeful smile on his face.

The game ended. There came a ragged countdown of the last seconds from the crowd, and the horn blared, and the crowd in the stands, already on its feet, exploded still again, and the Truckers' players from the bench exploded onto the floor, running madly, jumping, shouting, swarming over the sweaty players who were swarming over each other in turn.

The Little M's were walking away, taking last looks at the clock and the score, to see if it was really over, if it was really true. Dale, moving to the bench with his teammates, saw Mr. Bothner out on the floor joining in the celebration, embracing his oldest son, in the midst of boys and girls from the stands, who, whatever the rules about street shoes, were also flooding over the floor. Coach Burke moved through the gathering mob on the floor, too, smiling, grabbing and slapping people, shaking hands with both of his hands.

At the bench with his teammates, Dale looked for his towel. A young boy, darting down out of the bleachers, suddenly, in passing, slapped at him with an open hand, cuffed his forearm as he flashed by, and Dale, drained, wondered what it was in their loss that made the boy think he could slap at him so freely.

There on the bench, to his surprise, Lloyd Coombs sat with his face in his hands, crying. Dale recovered his towel, wiped his face. Then he said, "Come on, Lloyd, it's okay, let's go." Lloyd glanced up, red-eyed, lifted from the bench and moved along, looking to the floor.

At the tunnel, entering, they left the gym and crowd and celebration behind.

Walking into the locker room, they remained silent. In their aisle, they either sat down, to stare, or opened a locker door, to begin the process of undressing, showering, dressing.

Lucky was sitting on the bench. "We had 'em," he said. "Season's over," Chub said. "Time for baseball."

Dale sat on the bench several feet along, sat and stared. If only they had been slaughtered. If only they had trailed throughout and lost by twenty points. But of course they had had it, and then they did not have it, and it was the worst of losses. He could have won it, he was thinking. One basket. That one basket, and he could have won it. That one pass he had thrown away.

The Bothners had beaten him. They had won. The two brothers. The father. They wouldn't have without Joe

Dillard, but they had him. They had won. It was all that mattered.

Dale sat staring before him. He sat as if waiting for his heart to grant him permission to live again. He sat with his head down and his arms on his legs. A thought came to him that the resumption of his pride had caused the loss. He had taken that shot. Missed. He had believed he could do it. The punch in the nose. A big mistake. Bad judgment.

"Don't second guess yourself," Lucky said.

Dale turned his head to look along the bench. Lucky, sitting there untying his shoes, smiled even as he looked grim and drained. "You read my mind," Dale said.

Dale still sat there. He did not have whatever it took to move, even as the others were heading away to take their showers. Lucky, he saw, on the periphery of his vision, had gotten to his feet and walked away.

Dale sat there still. The Truckers had stormed in a moment ago, were slamming locker doors and heading off, too, to the gang shower at the end of the room. Dale still sat there. He had no wish to see any of them, to see the looks in their eyes, to be seen in any way or spoken to. His nakedness, it seemed, would be apparent to all. Something else, he knew, kept him sitting on the bench. Defeat. Disappointment. Defeat.

In time, not remembering having told himself to do so, Dale was standing to undo the lock on his locker, thinking that anyone, looking at him, would see that he was okay, that he knew it was just a game and it was over now. The season was over. He did not want anyone to think that he had really been defeated.

Locker opened, however, he sat back down on the bench. He looked toward the bottom of the locker, where before he had merely stared into a space before his nose.

"We went sixteen and one," Lloyd said. "We had a great year."

"Yeah, we did," Dale said. He had turned his head a little toward Lloyd but not enough for Lloyd to see his face.

Dale reached into the dark bottom of his locker, for no reason than to inform some imagined observer that he was okay, he was just moving slowly right now. Don't think he had really been beaten. He was okay.

He bent over to untie his shoelaces, to make it apparent to other imagined persons that he knew it was just a game. Someone, back from showering, passed, moist and steamy warm just behind him, making him feel how sticky sweaty he remained. Still, he thought he could sit there a while longer without anyone thinking that anything was wrong.

The Little M's, but for himself, had made their way over in a couple cars, and they would be leaving together to make the trip back. They'd leave it all behind, Dale knew, and he thought what a comfort it would be to be going with them. He wished he could. He no longer belonged here.

He removed a shoe, removed a warm sock, tossed them down. He removed the other shoe, tossed it down. He kept staring, looking, waiting, it seemed, for something to sprout, to give him a sign, a direction to take.

The Little M's, showered and dressed, were in their last stages of stuffing towels and socks into gym bags, preparing to head out. Lucky and Grady had cigarettes in their mouths now, puffing casually as they stuffed and zipped bags.

"Wheeler, you gonna sit there forever?" Chub said.

"Oh, I'll be in the shower in a minute," Dale said.

"Y'all ready to hit the road?" Lucky said to the others.

They were slipping on their expensive overcoats, taking up their bags, about to leave when a man appeared at the end of the aisle—Hal Doyle's father, Dale knew—sniffing at the certain smell.

"You're smoking in here!" he said, pointing at Lucky. "Put that cigarette out, young man, right now!"

Lucky smiled, placed his gym bag back on the bench, as if something this afternoon had finally gone his way. "Tell you what," he said in a friendly voice. "Why don't you step over here and make me do it. Be my guest."

All were quiet, motionless, as they paused to witness the man's response.

He appeared to think better of it; he did not move.

"What do you say?" Lucky said. "You want me to step out there? Would you like that—you small stack a shit?"

The man moved away. The other Little M's stifled modest laughter. "Guy's not dumb," Chub said. "I've seen Lucky like that; he'd of killed that dumb sonofabitch."

They moved again. They picked up bags, a last locker door was slammed. This was it.

"Dale, you gonna be okay?" Grady said.

"Yeah," Dale said.

"You think there's gonna be trouble, we'll stay," Lucky said.

"It's okay," Dale said. "Any second now I'm going to get moving. I'm okay."

"Hey, it was a good year," Grady said.

"Yeah, it was a good year," they all said, Dale included.

"Listen, see you around," Lucky said.

They stood there in their handsome coats, hair damp, combed into careful duck's tails. "Yeah, see you," Dale said, getting to his feet. "See you around."

They filed away, out along the main aisle. Their voices moved from the locker room and they were gone. Dale sat back down. He rested his elbows on his thighs, rested his forehead in his hands. He felt a little better now. There were no more voices, nor any running-water sounds, and he guessed he was the only one still in the locker room.

Then he sensed, knew, that someone had appeared at the end of the aisle. He expected to turn and see Slim, the locker room man, but looking over, there was Mr. Bothner, filling much of the space, looking at him.

"Fella, how's it going?"

Dale could not say, and he only looked back at the man, without expression.

"I just wanted to say good game."

Dale simply looked, and perhaps he meant to speak, but nothing came out. His face felt like a piece of glass which would break if he spoke, but even as he opened his gummy lips to say something, no words came out.

In June, when school was out for the summer, Dale bought cigarettes for the first time. Smoking seemed to have been beckoning to him for months, and even as he felt diminished making the purchase, something in the act was satisfying, too. It seemed to be who he was, who he had been becoming for some time now.

It was a warm summer evening, just turning dark at eight-thirty, and he was walking with nowhere to go. Nights like this the previous summer he had played endless basketball outdoors under the lights, game after game, dream after dream, unto a lather, and even as he believed still, somewhere within, that he would get it together and go out for basketball in high school, somewhere within he knew that everything was different now. He had believed that he could turn things around playing basketball. It hadn't happened.

He decided on his father's brand, Camels, and he decided to do so over a counter, at Peck's Drugstore in lower downtown. Refused, he could always use a machine. He did things on his own. He thought of things.

Thus, he entered the store, placed a dollar on the glass. "Camels," he said.

The clerk hardly looked up as he removed a package from a rack, a book of matches from a box, and placed them on the counter. Dale picked up the cigarettes, took the change in his other hand. It was then, as he turned to leave, that he imagined Miss Turbush standing there watching him.

For a moment, leaving the store and walking along the sidewalk, he no longer wanted a cigarette. Now that he had them, having them seemed enough. What he wanted was to go back in his life, to long ago, rather than ahead.

He took his time, walked along. Car lights and neon signs were on and there was blue haze overhead in the downtown air. He paused at a corner and did not cross with the light. He was going to stand for a moment, as older men stood at the curb on summer nights. He could understand things now he had not been able to understand a year or so ago, he thought. Lots of things.

The cigarettes maintained a presence in his shirt pocket as he walked again. The air had no chill at all tonight, even though it was just about dark by now. Summertime downtown. A scattering of people moved along the wide sidewalk. They glanced to store windows, to cars passing, to other people. Or they looked ahead, into the space they were walking into step by step.

Miss Turbush would speak against the cigarettes, he thought. She would try to talk him out of it. Of all things, he thought, he wished she were here now. Who would believe it? He wished his white-haired teacher was with him and he knew why, too. Because she made him feel real. They could stop at a diner, and drink root beer and talk. They could sit in a booth. He could introduce her to Lucky and Grady, or any of the Little M's, and she would have them listening and talking, would make them laugh, and they would like her as much as he liked her. She would make them feel real too.

Dale stood near an unlighted plate glass window to open

the pack. Finding the end of the gold band, he pulled it so it cut smoothly through the cellophane, all the way around the package, and came free with the top of the wrapper. Next, as he had seen others do, he tore back two triangles of tin foil, opened the folds, and tore them off. There were the tobacco ends of the packed cigarettes. He wanted to be, had to be now, he thought, as defiant and strong as Lucky and Grady and Chub, and maybe that was something he'd try to explain to Miss Turbush. He had to be like that, he'd tell her, and not like those who were on the other side, who cheated and tried to tell everybody what to do.

As much as he was interested in the act itself, he was interested in seeing how it looked. As he pushed up a Camel and drew it out, fresh and firm, and placed it in his lips, smelled the tobacco odor, he looked to the reflection in the glass, to the image of himself with the white object at its center. There it was. There he was. Once you started you couldn't ever quit, everyone said, but it wasn't anything he exactly believed or cared about right now.

The cigarette paper was sticking to his lower lip. As he pulled it free, it seemed to leave a bit of paper, to take away a piece of skin. Cigarette in his fingers, he used his tongue to work free the bit of paper, to soothe his lip and wash over the faint taste of blood. He would do it anyway, he thought, even if Miss Turbush tried to talk him out of it. And he would be right this time. And she would know he was right and would say so.

Moistening his lips, he repositioned the cigarette and removed the book of matches from his pocket. He wished, believed for the moment, that he might always be one upon whom friends could count. Don't worry, they would say. No matter what happens, Dale Wheeler won't go off and leave you in trouble. If you go down in battle and against any odds, he will think of something and will stay with you.

He struck the match, cupped his hands, and pulled some

dry smoke into his mouth. He flicked away the match, *whooohed* the smoke without inhaling. He felt at home in his heart as he stood there smoking. It was who he was and what he had been looking for. Being himself. He decided to take being himself as his code. Never to play their game. He was this person. The task was never to be them. Not ever.